Enrollment Form

☐ *Yes!* I WANT TO BE A *PRIVILEGED WOMAN*.
Enclosed is one *PAGES & PRIVILEGES™* Proof of
Purchase from any Harlequin or Silhouette book currently for
sale in stores (Proofs of Purchase are found on the back pages
of books) and the store cash register receipt. Please enroll me
in *PAGES & PRIVILEGES™*. Send my Welcome Kit and FREE
Gifts – and activate my FREE benefits – immediately.

More great gifts and benefits to come.

▼ DETACH HERE AND MAIL TODAY! ▼

NAME (please print)
_____

ADDRESS _____ APT. NO

CITY _____ STATE _____ ZIP/POSTAL CODE

PROOF OF PURCHASE ONLY

**NO CLUB!
NO COMMITMENT!**
*Just one purchase brings
you great Free Gifts and
Benefits!*

Please allow 6-8 weeks for delivery. Quantities are limited. We reserve the right to
substitute items. Enroll before October 31, 1995 and receive one full year of benefits.

Name of store where this book was purchased_____

Date of purchase_____

Type of store:

☐ Bookstore   ☐ Supermarket   ☐ Drugstore
☐ Dept. or discount store (e.g. K-Mart or Walmart)
☐ Other (specify)_____

Which Harlequin or Silhouette series do you usually read?
_____

Complete and mail with one Proof of Purchase and store receipt to:
U.S.: *PAGES & PRIVILEGES™*, P.O. Box 1960, Danbury, CT 06813-1960
Canada: *PAGES & PRIVILEGES™*, 49-6A The Donway West, P.O. 813,
North York, ON M3C 2E8

SD-PP5B

Rye Swept Her Into His Arms. "Nuzzle."

"Excuse me?" Paige asked, aghast at her present position.

"I said, 'Nuzzle me.' If you don't, I'm going to kiss you. We're being watched."

She glanced around. "I don't see anyone. Who cares anyway?"

"A white-haired lady in a pink bathrobe has focused her romantic little heart our way. Dammit, Paige, nuzzle—"

"Tell me why I should," she said quickly, restraining him as she hoped the right amount of mutiny rang in her voice.

Rye turned a triumphant grin on her. "Because we are about to enter the honeymoon cottage. Now, nuzzle!"

Paige buried her face against his neck, and she smelled leather and...pure, unadulterated male. He breathed a regular rhythm, apparently unaffected by her. She wished she could say the same for herself. No one had ever swept her off her feet before—literally or figuratively.

Dear Reader,

Are you looking for books that are fresh, sexy, and wonderfully romantic? Then look no more, because you've got one of them in your hands right now! Silhouette Desire, where man meets woman...and love is the result.

When you enter the world of Silhouette Desire, you travel to places where the hero is passionate...ready to do *anything* to capture the eternal affections of the heroine. He's a guy you can't help but fall a little in love with yourself...just as the heroine does. And the heroine—whether she's a full-time mom or full-time career woman—is someone you can relate to!

And in Silhouette Desire you'll find some of romance fiction's finest writers. This month alone we have Dixie Browning, Lucy Gordon, BJ James, Susan Crosby, Judith McWilliams and Ryanne Corey. And where else, but in Silhouette Desire, will you find the *Man of the Month* or a bold, sensuous new miniseries such as MEN OF THE BLACK WATCH?

Silhouette Desire is simply *the* best in romance...this month and every month! So, enjoy....

Sincerely,

Lucia Macro
Senior Editor

Please address questions and book requests to:
Silhouette Reader Service
U.S.: 3010 Walden Ave., P.O. Box 1325, Buffalo, NY 14269
Canadian: P.O. Box 609, Fort Erie, Ont. L2A 5X3

SUSAN CROSBY
ALMOST A HONEYMOON

SILHOUETTE *Desire*

Published by Silhouette Books

America's Publisher of Contemporary Romance

SILHOUETTE BOOKS

ISBN 0-373-05952-3

ALMOST A HONEYMOON

Printed in U.S.A.

Books by Susan Crosby

Silhouette Desire

The Mating Game #888
Almost a Honeymoon #952

SUSAN CROSBY

is fascinated by the special and complex communication of courtship, and so she burrows in her office to dream up warm, strong heroes and good-hearted, self-reliant heroines to satisfy her own love of happy endings.

She and her husband have two grown sons and live in the Central Valley of California. She spent a mere seven and a half years getting through college and finally earned a B.A. in English a few years ago. She has worked as a synchronized swimming instructor, a personnel interviewer at a toy factory and a trucking company manager. Involved for many years behind the scenes in a local community theater, she has made only one stage appearance—as the rear end of a camel! Variety, she says, makes for more interesting novels.

Readers are welcome to write to her at P.O. Box 1836, Lodi, CA 95241.

To Melissa Jeglinski, who provides focus, encouragement and laughs. I hate it when you're right! And to Harold & Ruth—I must have been in the "lucky" line when they handed out in-laws. You've been the cherry on top of my hot fudge sundae. I love you both.

One

He had been watching her for seven hours, since she'd left her Charlestown brownstone and taken a cab to Boston's Logan airport. Maintaining a discreet distance, he'd kept her in sight as they checked in at the airlines, then they passed the next half hour in the club lounge, where he feigned interest in a paperback murder mystery as she tapped efficiently on her laptop computer, oblivious to his watchful eye. She spoke with only one person at length, engaging in a subdued debate with a fellow laptop user about spread-sheet software.

Shortly before takeoff, she gathered her belongings, and he trailed her to the airplane, his gaze touching every person, calculating who might interfere with the successful completion of his newest assignment.

Now they were a little over an hour from touchdown at San Francisco International. He'd used the long hours to append his personal knowledge of her and the written information he'd been given the day before. The facts—Paige

O'Halloran, twenty-eight years old, the only child of Patrick O'Halloran, owner of the third largest shipping line out of Boston; graduated first in her class from Smith College, earned her MBA at Harvard; employed in her father's firm for five years—current position, comptroller.

Another fact—she'd recently done something completely out of character for her, the results of which were still toppling dominoes.

From his vantage point across the aisle and one seat back from her he had passed the time by adding his own observations to the dossier he'd been given. He deduced that she was accustomed to traveling, because the moment she took her seat, she slipped off her high heels and donned soft ballet-style slippers. She ignored the movie to instead work on her computer, and no amount of turbulence fazed her. She simply steadied her computer with one hand and continued to enter information with the other. She carried no bestseller to while away the hours, instead flipped through *U.S. News & World Report*.

She visited the rest room twice during the flight, and he noticed with no small degree of surprise that her dark green skirt and ivory blouse never wrinkled; her medium brown hair didn't droop a fraction from its elegant French twist; her makeup didn't fade, except for her lipstick, which she replaced several times with the same bronze hue. She put her seat back once during the long flight, resting her eyes, but hadn't slept. She chose the vegetarian entrée off the menu, consumed a glass of California Chardonnay, and finished everything on her tray except the two chocolate truffles packaged in a tiny box, which she dropped into her briefcase. She never failed to thank the flight attendant for his service and smiled as she made eye contact.

Her actions bespoke self-assurance and control, exactly as he had expected.

Conversely, her physical self seemed delicate, almost fragile, like a finely carved cameo, which he *hadn't* expected. Although above average in height for a woman, she was small boned and pale skinned, as if easily bruised or broken. Her body was shaped more like a freeway than a mountain road—until she turned around. What she lacked in curves up front she more than made up for in the backside, her rear being nicely rounded, upside-down-heart shaped and full, her long legs the reason high heels were created.

In short, Paige O'Halloran was a woman who generally blended in with the background. Her first impression was probably no impression. Excluding the tantalizing view she offered walking away, there was nothing special to draw the eye, nothing in her mannerisms to call attention to herself, nothing that said, "Look at me. I'm special."

If he hadn't known about her "unfortunate adventure," he would have guessed she was perfectly content with her life. But she had ruptured that image with her one indiscretion—and that made her intriguing, a dangerous pull in his line of work, in which allowing himself to be intrigued could mean personal disaster.

The cabin lights came on abruptly, a silent announcement of their imminent arrival. As passengers stirred, he made a quick trip to the rest room before the flight attendant served a light snack. On his return the subject of his observation dropped a floppy disk into the aisle as she packed away her computer.

He crouched to retrieve it, then paused as her scent drifted over him. He'd been blessed—or cursed, he couldn't decide which—with exceptionally keen senses, but his sense of smell was extraordinary. Recognizing a person's scent, even masked artificially with fragrance, had saved his hide uncounted times. He knew the smell of fear, sometimes subtle, sometimes overwhelming. He knew the smell of arousal. He had identified and mentally cataloged a staggering number of perfumes, colognes and after-shave lotions.

He couldn't, however, identify her perfume—and that bothered the hell out of him. He breathed in several times, committing it to memory, but the fact he couldn't give it a name irritated him; he arranged facts and observations in his mental file cabinet in alphabetical, chronological and logical order, and he liked it that way. But he could identify only elements of her perfume—an undertone of jasmine, a whiff of...rose? Maybe. But the overall effect was not exclusively floral. He'd figure it out later; he would have plenty of time.

He started to hand her floppy disk to her when his gaze settled on a subtle wrinkle of fabric along her thigh. A garter. This controlled, efficient, orderly woman wore a garter belt?

Shattered. All his perceptions of her were broken by that knowledge. Paige O'Halloran was a panty hose kind of woman; he would have bet his ample financial portfolio on it.

Her hand came into view, extended to receive the disk from him, and he noted short, unpolished fingernails, a clue to her steady use of a computer keyboard, no doubt, especially the smaller keys on laptops, but also indicative of her no-nonsense personality. He felt more comfortable slotting her into that pigeonhole.

"Thank you," she said, her gaze sending a silent question his way as he delayed returning her disk.

Her eyes, he noted, were a kind of marbled hazel, more green than blue. Or was it the green eye shadow she wore that made them seem that way?

Mumbling something reminiscent of "You're welcome," he returned to his seat, willing his thoughts away from the perfume he couldn't identify and the damned garter belt he couldn't reconcile with the woman. He couldn't allow himself any mental diversions.

He had orders to follow.

Paige O'Halloran slowed her steps when she spotted the uniformed man holding up a sign neatly penned with O'Halloran as she entered the terminal at the San Francisco airport. She approached the short, brawny man and identified herself.

"Are you waiting for me or another—"

"You, miss."

She observed the placid expression on the fifty-something man who looked more like a boxer than a chauffeur. She didn't take comfort in the once-broken-but-not-properly-set nose or the scar-tissue ridges scattered across his face. "I didn't order a limousine."

The man pulled a folded piece of paper from his pocket and passed it to her—a fax on O'Halloran Shipping letterhead, signed by her father, authorizing her pickup from the airport.

"I'll accompany you to the baggage area, miss. If you would identify your luggage for me, I'll take it from there." He wrestled her briefcase and computer pack from her resisting hands, then he turned from her, indicating with a hitch of his head that she should follow.

It wasn't her birthday, so why had her father arranged this surprise? She felt guilty enough having to fly first class this trip, but her need for space to prepare for the three upcoming meetings and her last-minute airline reservation had necessitated it. Her father knew she watched every penny of company expenses, never granting herself any luxuries she wouldn't allow another employee. She called it streamlining the budget; he called it being unnecessarily tightfisted. But Paige remembered their almost endless years of struggling better than he did.

Standing beside the baggage carousel, she tapped her fingertips together, not knowing what to do with her hands, missing the familiar appendage of her briefcase. The small purse that held little more than her wallet and keys hung lightly from her shoulder, not requiring attention. She satisfied herself that her precious bags were safe with the driver, then her gaze strayed around the baggage claim area. It was close to nine o'clock at night, but midnight Boston time. People stood yawning and stretching, shifting foot to foot as they waited for their luggage to appear.

Her glance settled on a man who stood directly across from her, noticeably motionless—the man who had picked up her floppy disk on the plane and returned it to her... finally. He was big. She hadn't realized how big, because on the plane he'd been crouched beside her. But she saw now how very tall he was—and *big*. A bodybuilder, undoubtedly. Military, she decided, eyeing the short haircut and smooth-shaven jaw. Except that he had a lone wolf sort of look to him. Something about him...

Sunglasses! He was wearing sunglasses on this, the shortest day of the year, at night. Talk about egotistical! Dismissing him with a toss of her head, she returned her glance to her bags before beginning a visual sweep of the cavernous area again—returning magnetically to the tall, still man.

He was a walking cliché, with his black leather jacket, black turtleneck shirt and unnecessary sunglasses, which hid what, judging from the angle of his head, was a blatant appraisal of a woman poured into a red minidress. His well-worn black jeans hugged contoured thighs and trailed long, sturdy legs, ending at—what a surprise—cowboy boots. She almost snorted at his predictability. *God save us from testosterone-riddled men.* At least he hadn't caught her looking at him, thus encouraging his bad-boy fantasies.

Still, there was something rather fascinating about the solid bulk of him—

Mraaap. A loud, deep tone alerted them to the jerky start of the carousel. Within seconds, suitcases began spilling over the edge. Her garment bag and Pullman were scooped up by the chauffeur when she identified them, then she exited the terminal, her driver loaded with bags, her own hands empty. She felt embarrassingly helpless, so unflatteringly feminine following the overburdened man.

She trailed him to a curiously unoccupied area alongside the terminal. No one milled around, not employees or passengers or security guards. She eyed the back of the man carrying her bags, a frisson of unwanted anticipation traveling down her. *Now, Paige,* she cautioned herself, *just because you don't like his looks doesn't mean he's a threat. Stop being paranoid.* Keeping herself beyond arm's reach, she watched his every move as he stowed her gear in the trunk.

A soft, repetitious squeak penetrated the night in rhythmic cadence. She squinted into the darkness, torn between watching the driver and trying to ascertain the source of the sound. Leather boots, perhaps? Every instinct snapped to attention as the tall man in black appeared out of nowhere.

He didn't have a suitcase—that fact struck her first. The same carryon bag that had been at his feet in the terminal now dangled from his hand, but he held no other luggage. Why had he been waiting at the carousel if he didn't have luggage?

"Miss?"

Paige cast a swift glance at the chauffeur, who stood beside the open back door of the limousine. Relieved, she scurried into the seat. Before she could find asylum within, he filled the space beside her. Him. The man in black, who smelled of leather and menace.

The door slammed shut before she could utter a sound, much less muster a scream. She made a quick grab for the opposite door—

"Electronic locks," he said as the handle wouldn't budge.

Her father's longtime fear for her surfaced. She had been kidnapped, really and truly kidnapped, after all. Digging deep for control, she fought the fear pulsating down her body as she faced her captor squarely. "Who are you? What do you want?"

He slid his dark glasses off and gave her a cool once-over. "Rye Warner. I'm your bodyguard."

Two

"**P**rove it," she told him. Proof was incidental—Paige recognized his voice, but she needed a little time to let the fear wash away completely.

The distinctive crinkle of leather sounded lightly in the confining space as he slid his wallet from inside his jacket, whisked out his driver's license and passed it to her. Then he focused a penlight on it, spotlighting the pertinent details.

Bryan Henry Warner. Sex, M; Hair, Brn; Eyes, Brn; Ht, 6-05; Wt, 240. She calculated his age at thirty-five. A pink donor circle clung to the upper left corner above an extremely flattering picture of the man. Bryan Warner, Rye to his business associates. But to her he was—

"Warner the Barbarian," she intoned as she flipped his license back to him.

"So, Harry, we meet at last."

Paige settled against the luxurious leather seat, glad that the darkness hid her wince at the obnoxious nickname he'd given her during one of their many phone conversations over the last two years. "Harry, short for harridan, meaning shrew," he had said pointedly, "although that's being generous."

Ignoring his taunt, she crossed her legs and smoothed the fabric of her skirt. "Why does my father think I need a bodyguard?"

"Patrick uncovered a plan to kidnap you."

She dropped her head back and groaned. "Not again. And you believed him? Look, Warner, my father has hired bodyguards for me three times in my life, each time believing I was ripe for a kidnapping."

"And?"

"There hasn't been a genuine threat yet."

"There is this time."

Thrown by the absolute assuredness in his tone, she stalled by looking out the window but saw little through the darkly tinted glass as they traveled through the city. She felt his gaze on her.

"Why you?" she asked.

"Probably because I'm the best."

She couldn't stop the soft snort of disbelief. "The most expensive, anyway."

"Now, Harry, we've quibbled about this for two years. My fees may be a little higher—"

"*Substantially* higher."

"But I do the job in half the time. In the end, you pay the same, probably less."

"It must be really tiresome lugging that ego around with you."

"And it must be a real drag following rules all the time," he countered.

Yes! she wanted to scream. But who would keep her father under control if she didn't enforce the rules and regulations? Who would keep the company from bankruptcy?

"So, who's allegedly after me this time?" she asked.

"Seems your fiancé got himself into a bit of financial trouble with the wrong people."

Paige stiffened. "I do not now have, nor have I ever had, a fiancé."

"Now there's a surprise," he muttered.

"Meaning?" The word skated across ice.

"Does the name Joey Falcon ring a bell?"

Joey Falcon, her fall from grace. She swallowed the embarrassment. "He asked me to marry him. I turned him down."

"He used you as collateral."

"How? And why would he?"

"Seems Falcon was on that cruise you took because he was hiding out from his . . . shall we call them creditors? He had a friend on the ship's staff who gave him a passenger list. He zeroed in on you."

"And here I've been thinking he fell for my charm and beauty." Sarcasm coated her words, the self-deprecation genuine and lifelong, as natural to her as breathing and as likely to change as it would be for her to stop breathing.

She didn't like a lot of change in her life, wasn't comfortable with it. The only way to keep control was to establish and stay with a routine, physically and mentally. She spent a lot of effort adhering to the structure she enforced on her daily life, starting with a half hour of yoga in the morning and ending with a half hour bubble bath at night.

The only time in her adult life when she hadn't followed that routine had resulted in disaster; she was sure she'd suffered a personality transformation for that single week recently because she'd substituted a walk on the deck of the cruise ship for her morning yoga, and dancing in the moonlight for her nighttime bubble bath.

Never again. She'd never, ever set aside the meditation and relaxation time she so desperately needed to maintain her inner peace merely for a frivolous moment of pleasure. Joey Falcon had cured her of that.

Paige sighed inwardly. She should have identified her restlessness before impulsively making reservations for a seven-day Caribbean cruise. She should have stopped and taken stock, written down and analyzed her reasons for going, then perhaps she wouldn't have been susceptible to the very charming Joey Falcon. But for the first time in her life she'd acted and reacted without first weighing the pros and cons. And for the first time in her life she was embarrassed by her behavior.

Joey had leaned his arms against the railing beside her as the ship left port and had rarely left her side in the ensuing days. Usually a woman who didn't command much notice, she was flattered by his attention, by the way he catered to her every whim. On the sixth day at sea he proposed, but by then reality had intruded. When he hadn't been exuding charm, she'd seen a glimpse of something else—something that had made her uneasy. At the least, he'd been insincere. At the most? Not frightening, exactly, but not trustworthy, either.

He had refused to believe she didn't want to continue seeing him and had called her daily for the past two weeks, had showered her with flowers and gifts. Her restlessness had been replaced with exasperation, followed by irritation, even a little fear.

"Actually, it's a relief to know Joey was only greedy," she said, breaking a long silence. "If he really was in love with me, I might never be rid of him. I assume he approached my father for the money."

Rye shook himself to attention. Knowing Lloyd was driving allowed him to relax his guard, but Paige's silence while she analyzed her situation had threatened to put him to sleep. "When Patrick refused to pay his debts," he said through a yawn, "Falcon informed him that he'd been given an extension on the loan based on your engagement and the potential money available. Now he's gone back into hiding, and his creditors want their money. Falcon insists they'll grab you for ransom."

"At least he warned us. That's more than I would have given him credit for doing."

"The report I saw indicates Falcon has major financial problems. Given a little more time, we should know in more detail what we're up against."

She shifted, impatient. "So I'm forced into hiding, too. Doesn't that make my father a target?"

"He's using a local security team."

"How long do I have to stay in San Francisco?"

"Until Falcon's been flushed out."

"What if my meetings are done earlier?"

"The meetings were a ruse. You really are in hiding, Paige. You're not to have contact with anyone but me. I'll be in touch with Patrick."

She held herself aloof, cool as a spring runoff, apparently unconcerned with the danger. But Rye knew her blood ran hotter than that. A little garter told him so.

And her "unfortunate adventure" told him that under that cool facade she craved excitement.

"Where are we going?" she asked. "To your home?"

"To a small, discreet hotel."

"Why San Francisco? I know you live here, but with only a little investigating, anyone could find out you work for us occasionally. If your reputation is as far-reaching as you'd like to believe—"

"I'm doing this as a favor to your father. He caught up with me by phone in London and begged me to help, so cut the insults, Paige. I landed at Logan, tracked you, then stayed awake the whole time watching over you. I'm tired."

"If you flew in from London, you should have luggage. Where is it?"

"Being held at the airport until Lloyd can get over to pick it up."

"This is idiotic! Why couldn't we just hide out somewhere near home?"

"Because I have work to do. I can stay with you and also catch up on what's been neglected while I've been gone."

"You'll be prorating your bill, I assume," she said, her voice dripping honey.

"What?"

"Well, it's only fair. Why should we pay while you work for other people?"

Rye didn't know whether to laugh or explode at her relentless guardianship of O'Halloran Shipping funds. "I won't be off the clock with you for a second, Harry."

Lloyd swung the car into a driveway, negotiated a narrow road around a three-story house-turned-hotel, then stopped in front of a small building. The headlights offered a quick glimpse of a brick cottage sheltered by a profusion of climbing ivy and low bushes before the beams were doused, leaving only a soft yellow glow coming from a porch light.

"Wait here," Rye ordered Paige before he left the car and followed the driver into the bungalow, which at one time served as a caretaker's housing. A low fire gleamed from the hearth, the light casting flickering shadows around the impeccably furnished living room. "Everything secure?" he asked Lloyd, who came up behind him and deposited suitcases on the plush carpet.

"As you requested, sir."

"Don't call me sir."

"Yes, sir."

Rye turned to look at the man, seeing past the scarred face and crooked nose to the strength of character beneath. The perpetually bland expression hid a wealth of feeling. "You did a great job, as usual, Lloyd. And on particularly short notice."

"Thank you, sir."

Rye shook his head, exasperated, as he inspected the rest of the cottage—a bedroom sporting a huge four-poster bed and a second fireplace, also lit, then a bathroom containing an oversize tub. "Looks good," he said.

"You may find the couch a bit confining."

"I noticed. I'm so tired it won't matter at this point. I may feel differently tomorrow night."

"Get some sleep. I'll watch from outside tonight."

"Thanks, old friend." He came very close to sighing. "Well, the princess awaits. I have a feeling it's going to be a long, long assignment."

"She doesn't seem to, ah, particularly care for you, sir."

"Ms. O'Halloran and I have a history of disagreement."

"She's quite attractive, if I may be so bold as to say."

"You think so? Maybe I can't see past the nitpicking Scrooge that I know her to be." He pressed a button on a palm-size remote control as he returned to the car, unlocking it.

"How dare you lock me in," Paige said, low and angry as she ignored his hand and slid out of the car.

"On the contrary, Harry, I was locking others out."

"Well, you took your sweet time coming back to get me."

"I wanted to check out the arrangements personally." He plucked her coat and purse from her hands and tossed them to Lloyd. Before she could take two steps, he swept her into his arms.

"What are you doing? Put me down!" She shoved at his shoulders.

"Nuzzle," he ordered her.

"Excuse me?" If frost could burn words, it had.

"I said nuzzle me. If you don't, I'm going to kiss you. Your choice."

"What are you talking about?"

"We're being watched."

Paige glanced around. "I don't see anyone. Who cares, anyway?"

"A white-haired lady in a pink bathrobe has focused her romantic little heart our way from the main house. Dammit, Harry, nuzzle—"

"Not in this lifetime."

"Don't say I didn't warn you." He tilted her his direction, bringing their faces close.

"Tell me why I should," she said quickly, restraining him as she hoped the right amount of mutiny rang in her voice.

He turned a triumphant grin on her. "Because we are about to enter the honeymoon cottage."

"You're jok—"

He closed the small gap between them, but she jerked away after the merest graze of lips.

"So help me, Harry—"

Paige buried her face against his neck, and she smelled leather and...pure, unadulterated male. He breathed a regular rhythm, apparently unaffected by her. She wished she could say the same for herself. She wanted to cling, although whether from fear or excitement, she didn't know. Both jockeyed for position. No one had swept her off her feet before, literally or figuratively.

"You can let go."

His words infiltrated the battle she'd begun to wage within. She loosened her hold as he set her down, her heels sinking into a lush carpet. He continued to hold her elbow as she wobbled briefly.

"You all right?" he asked.

"Yes, of course. Why wouldn't I be?" Her gaze took in the loveliness of the room, with its English countryside motif and warm, deep colors.

"You seemed to enjoy your role, *wife*."

Paige ignored his grin. "I'm not stupid, Warner. I know it's to my advantage to play the game."

"Do you take that much convincing in bed, too?"

Paige gaped at his audacity.

"Personally, I *like* a challenge," he continued.

"You smug, self-centered—"

Lloyd cleared his throat and stepped into the fray. "Miss O'Halloran, I've placed your bags in the bedroom. Is there anything I can get you before I go?"

The momentary cease-fire helped Paige find her center of control again. She turned slowly to the driver and extended her hand. "Please call me Paige. And you are?"

He accepted the gesture of friendliness. "Lloyd, Miss O'Halloran. A light snack awaits you, as you can see. I didn't know your preference of beverage, so you'll find a variety to choose from. If there's nothing further?''

"Not unless you can snap your fingers and have this mess disappear.''

"Good night, then.'' He touched two fingers to his forehead in salute. "Sir."

Rye roused himself to say goodbye. He was so tired he could hardly stand. And Paige wasn't making his life any easier. He watched her lift the cellophane off a tray of fruit and grab a bunch of red grapes before seating herself on the couch. He eyed the sofa hungrily, starved for sleep. His gaze shifted as she crossed one leg over the other. She arched her foot until her shoe fell to the floor, recrossed her legs and rid herself of the other shoe, then bounced her foot rhythmically as she popped one grape after another into her mouth. Her chewing slowed as she caught him staring.

"What?'' she asked, the belligerent tone bringing him back to awareness.

Ignoring her, he slid out of his jacket and hung it on the back of a chair. Slowly, he moved to fix himself a plate of fruit, cheese and crackers. He uncorked a bottle of cabernet sauvignon and poured a glass. "Want some?''

No answer. He turned around and found her staring at the weapon tucked into the waistband of his jeans.

She lifted her gaze. "Where did you get that? You couldn't have had it on the plane.''

"Lloyd passed it to me as I climbed into the car. The holster's in my bag. Why? Do guns bother you?''

"I've never known anyone who had one. I guess it makes everything seem so real.''

"I don't waste my time on games, Harry. Wine?''

"Umm, yeah. Thanks. I guess I should have offered you some food. Sorry. I can't quite assimilate all of this yet.''

He passed her the glass. "Just work with me, Paige. I'll try to make this as painless as possible. Maybe after we've spent a few days together, we'll find a way to—''

"Days?'' she repeated. "How many days?''

"I couldn't even guess."

"But what about . . ."

He sat beside her and sipped his wine before placing it on the low table before them. "What about what?"

"Christmas. It's only four days away."

Her voice seemed suddenly small and faraway. He wondered at it, and at the expression that settled on her face, worry mixed with hurt. A Scrooge who likes Christmas? Deciding not to taunt her with the observation, he instead held his plate toward her. "Have some, if you want. We may have you back in time for Christmas. I can't make any promises."

She absently picked up a slice of Cheddar and nibbled on it. "I have to be home for Christmas," she said softly, adamantly, after a minute of silence.

Rye shook his head. He really needed sleep. He devoured the rest of the food then stood and returned the empty plate to the table. "I can't hold my eyes open. I'm going to sleep on the couch. Lloyd will be outside for tonight, so don't worry about anything."

"I guess I'm being sent to bed." She stood, sweeping up her shoes as she did so.

He brushed by her to use the bathroom, and she filled her wineglass and fixed herself a plate of food while he was gone before retreating with it to the bedroom, elbowing the door shut as he dropped a blanket and pillow on the sofa.

"Don't use the telephone," he cautioned just as the door clicked shut.

She pulled it open after a few seconds, having divested herself of the food and wine. "Why not?"

"There's a lot of sophisticated tracing equipment out there. One call, and your location could be pinpointed."

"I want to call my father."

"It's after one o'clock in Boston."

"So?"

"Don't you think he'll be asleep?"

"*So?*"

Rye opened a suitcase Lloyd had packed for him and pulled out a T-shirt and sweatpants. "This isn't his fault, Harry. He's been notified we're here. Let him sleep."

She took several long strides into the room. "Why should I? Why the *hell* should I? He's treating me like a child! Why didn't he tell me what was going on? He hired you without so much as a hint to me, his very adult daughter. And you, *you* dragged out the charade, letting me think I was in danger from *you*. I'll bet you got a real kick out of that, didn't you?"

He stood there listening but not hearing. Promises of sleep buzzed in his ears then rolled in waves down to his toes. He pulled his gun from his waistband and set it on the table beside the couch. "We'll talk in the morning."

She lifted her hands and laughed without humor at the ceiling. "I see. Another Patrick O'Halloran, are you? Your timetable. Your rules."

"Paige—" He dropped onto the sofa.

"Your tone is quite clear, Warner. 'Pity the poor emotional woman. She doesn't know what she's doing.' I've got news for you—I can damn well take care of myself."

One boot fell to the carpet, then the other. He stood and turned to face her squarely. Her belligerent pose almost drew a smile, but he held it back, figuring she would hurl another accusation at him. "Look, Harry, I've had about four hours of sleep in the last forty-eight. I can't deal with you right now." He peeled his turtleneck over his head; he moved his hands to his belt buckle. "Now, you can stay here and watch if you want. I'm not particularly modest. But it would kind of shatter our *professional* relationship, don't you think?"

Three

Her gaze wandered over him, dispassionately at first, then with interest. He saw the change as it unfolded, was unwillingly flattered by it, but shoved it aside. Resolutely, he unbuttoned his jeans, expecting her to run off. She didn't budge. Her steady observation began to burn him, a core of heat that pooled low and fiery and spread through his limbs. She swallowed; he battled a desert-dry mouth.

He hooked his thumbs in the waist of his jeans and inched them down. "Sorry, I don't have the finesse of an exotic dancer—"

Her eyes widened, as if finally aware of what she was seeing. He shoved the jeans down and off. The black cotton briefs covered the essentials, although not for much longer if she didn't avert her eyes soon.

"Seen enough?" he queried.

She flashed a wicked smile and spun away, tossing her final words over her shoulder. "Great socks, Warner."

Rye glanced down at his feet as the door clicked shut. Goofy stared up at him, his sister's last birthday gift to him. Grinning, he pulled them off and slid into the sweatpants and T-shirt. He heard the sound of the bathtub being filled, then nothing.

Paige rested her wineglass on the edge of the tub and eased into the bubble-layered heat. Instantly soothed, she sighed. Physically exhausted but mentally wide-awake, she sipped her wine and faced the reality of her predicament, which seemed far more serious than she had thought at first. Rye's presence should have been indication enough. He was never called in for light security work. He charged exorbitant fees and earned them; there was no man her father admired more. Long before she'd had contact with him, she'd heard tales of his exploits, tales so vivid he'd seemed like a mythical figure out of an action movie, tales, she'd suspected previously, rather like those of a fisherman describing the one that got away, a ten-inch fish taking on sharklike dimensions in the reenactment.

Rye Warner was no ten-inch fish. He was muscle head to toe and unafraid to show himself off. She hated brawny men, had always believed they were among the most egotistical people on earth. Who wouldn't be when they spent hours every day preening in front of a mirror, admiring their own bodies? No, thanks. She'd take a thoughtful, sensitive man any day.

Right, Paige. Like Joey Falcon? She dropped her head back against the rim of the tub. He'd been romantic and charming, complimenting her constantly, always bringing her gifts, holding doors open, pulling out chairs—where had that gotten her? Of course, Rye sat on the other end of the scale. He probably didn't have a romantic bone in his body, was the kind of man who wouldn't slow down for a woman walking in high heels—the kind of man to flex his substantial muscles at the slightest twinkle in a woman's eye.

Well, he wouldn't find *her* a panting, drooling, stammering admirer. He could take his overdone pectorals and deltoids, and his bulked-up biceps and triceps, cover his rock hard buns and his...masculinity with a skimpy nylon bathing suit, oil up his rippling body and—

The image suddenly didn't seem so disgusting. *Quick, change the picture.* Rye posed in front of an audience, his arms curled, one up, one down, his head twisted to one side, women screaming. *There! That's better.* Egotistical jerk.

She would have to tread carefully with him. He pushed her buttons too easily, had done so from the first phone conversation she'd ever had with him, when she'd called to tell him he had to submit a detailed expense report, not simply an all-inclusive invoice for his expenses. It had been all downhill since, their rousing discussions sizzling across telephone wires. He had managed to do what no one else ever had. He'd made her lose her temper.

Until Warner the Barbarian had come into her life, she hadn't gotten angry—ever.

Rages were her father's expertise.

Snuggling deeper under the comforter, Paige ignored the sound of the shower running. Sharing a hotel room—or any room—with a man was unnerving. Her mind's eye could picture the oversize man in the large tub, could picture the brass fixture he'd have to duck his head under to rinse shampoo away and the frilly shower curtain pulled around the curved rod overhead, vivid contrast to his utter maleness.

She had awakened half an hour ago, forced herself to complete her morning ritual of yoga and meditation, then had climbed back into bed when she heard Rye open the door from the living room that accessed the bathroom. She had slept ten hours, minus the times she woke after disjointed dreams starring her father, Rye and Joey in which she did a lot of running and hiding while they all searched her out.

The shower water cut off, and a variety of new sounds had her speculating on what he was doing. The silence of toweling off, the tap of metal against porcelain as he shaved, sixty seconds of blow-drying his hair, the rustle of fabric and jangle of a belt buckle as he dressed. She glanced at the bedside clock. Thirteen minutes, beginning to end, and he was done.

When she heard the latch of the door open and close, she began her own hour-long routine, eventually emerging from the room dressed in a royal blue wool skirt and pastel blue silk shell.

"Good morning," she said as she entered the living room, determined to get off on the right foot with him today. He was seated on the sofa, a steaming cup of coffee in one hand, a pen in the other. A yellow legal pad contained a list of numbered items that she couldn't read upside down.

"You're not going anywhere."

Paige crossed her arms over her chest and bit back a stinging response. "Did I ask?"

"You're dressed up."

"Pardon me. If I'd known I was going to be in need of them, I would have packed my prison blues. I was under the mistaken impression that I was here to attend business meetings." She cocked her head at him. "Did you get up on the wrong side of the sofa?"

He slouched against the cushions and blew out a long breath. "Sorry. I had trouble sleeping. It's been a grueling couple of weeks." He jerked a thumb over his shoulder. "Coffee's hot. Lloyd also brought pastries and fruit."

After Paige served herself, she took a seat in a chair opposite him to use the same low table. "I want to talk to my father."

"Any time. I have to route the call through another number."

"How do I transmit data from my computer to the office?"

"You can't."

"But—"

"Think of this as a vacation, Harry."

"And I'm supposed to fill my time watching you work? How exciting." She bit into an almond-sprinkled bear claw and closed her eyes in appreciation as she savored the richness. She caught him staring at her, and looked down, expecting crumbs on her blouse or something. "What?"

He dropped his glance to the paper in front of him. "Nothing."

She brushed the corners of her mouth, found no trace of food, then shrugged off his odd gaze. "Can't we compromise in some way? I can't just sit all day watching television. I'll go nuts."

"Do you have a printer?"

"No. I transmit by modem."

"If I arrange for a printer, you could run things off, and I could have Lloyd fax them to your office, through another source, of course."

"That's fine for sending. What about receiving?"

"If you can figure something out, I'll arrange it."

His eyes focused on her mouth again, disconcerting her, making it difficult to swallow. She couldn't get a handle on him this morning. He was distracted and intensely focused at the same time.

"Was the bed comfortable?" he asked as he wrote something else on the paper.

Her mouth curved teasingly. "Heavenly. It's so *big*. I had plenty of room to stretch out and—"

He lifted his head. "This *is* the honeymoon cottage."

"There was certainly room for two."

He rooted her to her seat with his gaze. "I don't suppose you'd consider trading beds? You'd fit on the couch a lot better than I do."

"At your daily rate, you can manage a little discomfort, Warner. So, does security loosen enough to allow for maid service, or should I make my bed?"

"Management has been asked not to disturb us."

"We can't go out at all? Not even to eat?"

"Lloyd will keep us fed. Anything you want, just ask."

"When does he sleep if he's catering to us plus being a night watchman?"

Rye picked up the telephone receiver and began punching numbers. "He won't be around every night. Just last night, because I was so tired."

"Meaning, we pay for an extra man because you came to this job tired. No wonder your bills are so outrageous."

"It's all relative, Harry. What value do you put on your life?"

Paige opened and closed her mouth. He'd stumped her with logic, leaving her no argument. She drummed her fingers on the upholstered arms of the chair as she watched him punch in another series of numbers, then sit back, the slightest smile on his lips. His gaze dropped to her legs as she crossed one over the other, and she felt a tremor of awareness at the unspoken flattery in his eyes, hardly able to comprehend that such a little action could spur Warner the Barbarian's interest.

"Warner here," he said into the telephone before tipping the mouthpiece and saying to Paige, "Do you ever wear miniskirts, or is your standard the middle-of-the-knee look you've got on?"

She watched him catalog her body, zone by zone, forcing her to analyze her response to his blatant appraisal. Her nipples drew instantly into hard buds against sheltering lace that became suddenly abrasive, almost painfully so. Could he see her reaction? If she crossed her arms over her chest, would he smirk with self-satisfaction?

The longer he stared, the more she ached—and the more uncomfortable she became. She had to know what he could see.

She leaned forward to pick up her coffee cup and sent a quick glance down herself. Damn. There was no way his eagle eyes could have missed *that*.

"I've been known to expose my knees," she forced herself to say into the heavy silence. "But since I work mostly with men, I have to be careful of the image I present."

"It's hard to imagine you letting down—" He jerked the receiver up again. "Patrick... No problems... Ask her yourself... All right, got it... Here, I'll put her on." He passed the phone to Paige.

"You all right, kid?" Patrick asked, after she said hello.

Paige welcomed the chance to divert her train of thought. "I'm furious with you."

"What do you think of Warner? Nice touch, huh?"

She watched Rye add another line to his growing list. *He's younger than I expected,* she thought. "As prison guards go, he rates a ten." She returned a placid stare to Rye's raised brows and a one-sided quirk of his mouth.

"He knows what he's doing. You can trust him."

"Well, I guess I'll have to, won't I? Why didn't you tell me about Joey? I'm not a child."

"But you're still my baby. You took care of me for a long time, honey. I'm just returning the favor."

Paige slumped a little. "We took care of each other, Dad. We grew up together, but we're both grown up now. I can handle the truth. Do you really believe I'm in that much danger?"

"Yes, I do."

"And you? What are you doing to protect yourself?"

"Security's solid, honey. Don't worry about me. Did Rye tell you not to call home?"

"Oh, yes. I got my orders." She unconsciously watched Rye as he moved to pour himself another cup of coffee. Comparing the width of his shoulders to the slenderness of his hips made her stomach flip-flop. She looked away, willing herself to remember his ego. "Are you sure I can't drum up some business while I'm here?"

"Rye says you need to lay low. He's the boss."

"What's happening with Collins-Abrahamson?"

"The deal's on hold until you get back."

"Promise?"

"Have I ever lied to you, kid?"

Paige laughed briefly. "That was a joke, right?"

He sputtered. "I haven't lied about anything important."

"How about the other bodyguards you arranged for me?"

"Now, Paige, honey. Those were just little white lies. They weren't meant to hurt you."

"Uh-huh. I'm really angry, Dad. Don't think we won't discuss this further when I get home."

"You'll forgive me."

"Don't be so sure. Will I talk to you soon?"

"Every day, kid. Relax, okay? Pretend you're on vacation."

"Did you and Warner conspire? That's exactly what *he* said. But as you'll both recall, it was my vacation that started this mess."

"We all make mistakes."

"Yeah, well, mine was a doozy."

"It'll turn out, kid. Keep the faith."

She cradled the receiver softly. "This is the worst possible time for me to be away."

"Why?" Rye finished the sentence he was writing, then looked up.

"We've got a big deal cooking, a potential merger. My father tends to take risks with the company he has no business taking. If I'm not there to intervene, I'm afraid of what will happen."

"Your father built that company on risks."

"But it's stable now. A lot of people depend on him for work. He has to be more careful." She stood and refilled her coffee cup before moving to stand by the mantel to stare at the fire. "It doesn't matter. He'll do what he wants anyway and tell me about it later."

"Don't you ever get messed up?"

She turned around. He had assumed a casual pose—one ankle crossed over his knee, his arm stretched along the back of the couch, a pencil dangling lightly from his fingers. She didn't like the way he studied her.

"What do you mean?"

He gestured with a quick hand. "I mean nothing on you wrinkles or clings or droops. Not a strand of hair out of place. Would any dare?"

Rye watched her pat her hair, was interested in the way she touched an item on the mantel and examined the details before inspecting the next curio. His nose twitched at the unnamed scent that trailed her as she moved around the room. He suddenly wished her hair wasn't so flawless, wanted to brush a loose strand behind her ear. Any excuse to touch her, to feel that little jolt between them that he chose to acknowledge and she probably chose to deny.

"Would you tell me about Falcon?" he asked.

"To what purpose?"

Rye grinned. "You must be dynamite in negotiations. Are you always so circumspect?"

"I can keep my own counsel, if that's what you mean. I don't let emotion interfere with the business at hand."

"Until Falcon," Rye said pointedly.

"Joey wasn't business."

He bowed his head. "Touché."

Paige lifted her coffee cup then set it back down. "Joey Falcon is terminally cute."

"Terminally cute." Rye tried not to choke on the words.

"And doggedly devoted."

"You *liked* that?"

"I don't psychoanalyze myself. I guess I thought it was what I wanted, at least briefly. I don't know. I don't really even care anymore. I just want him out of my life for good."

"That's a real possibility, depending on who catches up with him first."

Paige winced. "I don't want him harmed. I just want him to stop being an albatross around my neck."

She watched Rye fix a plate of food for himself and shook her head at his offer to get her something. The silence between them stretched uncomfortably.

"I was surprised when I found out your age," he said at last. "Patrick is forty-six, right? That means he was eighteen when you were born."

She embraced the sudden change of subject. "My mother was seventeen."

He approached the hearth to stand beside her. "That's what you meant when you said you grew up together. Sorry, I didn't mean to eavesdrop..."

"My mother died when I was four. Her family had never accepted their marriage, so my parents had moved in with my dad's father, supposedly just until Dad could finish high school. Grandad was the one who started O'Halloran Shipping. When he passed away—I was six, I think—the business was almost bankrupt. My father turned it around."

"More than that. What kind of price did *you* pay?"

"Me?" Paige was startled. No one had ever questioned what she had given up through the years.

"A young father, a growing business demanding every minute of his time. Did you pass from one baby-sitter to another, one housekeeper to another?"

"I grew up at my father's feet. The first few years, whenever I wasn't in school, I was at the office, or following him to the docks, or traveling with him to sign deals. We made an apartment out of some office space, then as the business boomed we bought a house. I worked for the firm in various capacities until I went off to college. He came home for a few hours' sleep each night."

"Sounds like he didn't have a social life."

"He didn't. He loved my mother beyond belief. Beyond sensibility, even. He still worships her memory." *One I will never live up to.*

"Are you like your mother?" he asked.

"I don't know. I have little memory of her, mostly things my father told me. I don't think I look like her, not from what Dad says, anyway."

"Don't you know what she looked like?"

"No. In a fit of rage shortly after her death he destroyed her pictures."

"Why?"

"I don't know."

"Didn't you ask?"

She shook her head briefly, sharply. She was tired and on edge, uncomfortable with the emotions surfacing. If she looked at Rye right now, she'd see sympathy. She didn't want sympathy.

"Tell me how you met my father," she said, lifting her coffee again.

His hesitation was brief and considering. "Patrick and I met when he and a few competitors discovered consistently short shipments on certain routes. I was hired to find the source."

"But how did my father know to call you?"

He lifted a shoulder in a brief shrug. "There is a labyrinth of information that filters among industrialists. They guard their contacts, yet they also share, especially regarding security. What affects one company often affects another."

"Keeping a lid on the information flow also keeps your identity a secret," Paige said. "Without anonymity you couldn't function as well."

Rye nodded. A jolt of awareness struck him, fascination with the way her mind worked. She cut through layers with knife-edged logic, and the revelation staggered him physically—a twist he could live without.

More in his favor, though, she wasn't a vulnerable woman. She was strong and in control, probably not as much in need of his protection as Patrick believed. It was important that she stay strong. If she showed one bit of weakness, his own vulnerability could surface. And that he needed to avoid at all costs.

"Listen, if you want to do some work, I've got calls to make," he said.

She drained her coffee cup and returned it to the lace-covered table. "How soon can Lloyd pick up a printer for me?"

"He'll call when he wakes up. Whatever you need, just tell him."

She picked up her computer pack and set it on the table beside the remnants of their breakfast. "What's the story on Lloyd? Is he an employee or what?"

"Or what."

She turned around. "Meaning?"

"I leave the telling of that story to Lloyd, if he so chooses. He's not an employee, but he helps me out sometimes."

"Is the limousine his or yours?"

"It's rented. Why?"

"The windows are tinted. We would be safe inside, wouldn't we? I can't stand the thought of being cooped up here."

Ending the conversation with a "We'll see," he picked up the telephone, leaving her to her own devices as he began a series of calls that required decoding to be fully understood. He spoke in the jargon of his business, words sprinkled with numbers, letters and abbreviations. He filled the yellow pad before him with page after page of notes. Part of her stayed tuned in to him because she admired the way he dealt with the business first then took a minute for the social niceties, remembering to ask about family members, health statuses, even special occasions.

He had never had a phone conversation like that with *her*. Resentment burrowed into her and built. What was she? Less than a human being to be treated as cavalierly as he had these last years? Why had she deserved less consideration than any other client?

When he made probably the tenth call in two hours, his voice changed. Softened. Took on a note of tenderness.

"Hi... I'm doin' great. How are you?... I've missed you, too. Are you feeling okay?... I'd be with you if I could, you know that... How's our little one?"

Our little one? The pencil in Paige's hands snapped. So, he has someone special in his life. A wife? Perhaps even a child? So what? And why does that surprise me? she thought, disgusted with herself. He's intelligent and attractive and successful, and he's proving right now that he can be tender. A lot of women probably like a macho superstud. *Not me, though.*

So why are you so disappointed? she asked herself. *Because a part of me—a tiny, almost insignificant part— wishes a man like that would be interested in me.* There! She'd said it. A moment of honesty. She'd dealt with it; now she could relegate it to the strongbox of lost dreams she kept locked in her head.

Thoughts of her mother escaped as she tried to close the lid. A perfect woman, according to her father. *The* perfect woman. Soft-spoken and soothing, a paragon of femininity. Paige had tried to emulate what she knew of her. Only Rye had broken through the wall of control she'd cultivated.

If she had learned nothing else from her debacle with Joey Falcon, she had figured out that she just wasn't herself right now. She had been feeling more than restlessness, more than a mild desire for something to happen. For the last year, she'd felt an urgent tug toward something unknown, a yearning to discover passion, not only physically but spiritually. She wanted to break out. But to what? How do you stop continually strolling down garden paths if no one ever invites you on a marathon?

You sign up, she admonished herself. She knew she had to take charge of her own destiny. She just didn't quite know how to do it, especially when she was being reminded by her father and Rye that she was powerless at the moment. Follow orders; we'll take care of you.

And she didn't recognize the person inside of her who just wanted to be taken care of.

Rye hung up the phone and stretched hugely. A glance at his watch confirmed what his stomach announced—that it was time for lunch. His gaze settled on Paige as she hunched over the too-high table her laptop sat on. She shifted her shoulders and rolled her head, easing unseen tension. Or was it really so unseen? As little as he had observed her, he was already able to pick up on her moods.

She would undoubtedly deny she *had* moods, of course, but he'd already seen several. Of them all, he most liked the playfulness he'd seen when she'd commented on his socks last night. He liked her belligerent side pretty well, too. Both made him laugh. He scrutinized her a little longer, pushed himself up from the couch and moved behind her.

When he settled his hands on her shoulders, she nearly jumped out of her seat.

"Don't sneak up on me," she ordered as she tugged herself forward.

He pushed his thumbs into the knotted muscle at the base of her neck and smiled at the involuntary groan he drew from her. "Should I stop?" he asked.

"No."

He grinned, deepening the massage, adding his fingers and palms. Her fragility startled him, making him ease the pressure. Her head drooped forward. "Hang tight a sec," he said. He swept up a pillow, instructing her to stand. Spinning the chair around, he laid the pillow over the chair back.

"Sit backward," he said. "Lay your head on the pillow."

She eyed her skirt, then the chair. Cautiously, she straddled the seat, but for every inch she lowered her body, her skirt raised an inch. She started to back off. "I don't think—"

"Harry, I've seen my share of female leg. It won't bother me."

"But—"

"Trust me."

Four

—————

Her skirt rode up, exposing the tops of nude-tone stockings, garters attached to strips of midnight blue satin and a few mouth-watering inches of skin. She plucked ineffectually at her hem while shifting her bottom, only succeeding in hiking her skirt higher.

"Leave it," he ordered, an unfamiliar hoarseness scraping the words along his throat.

Stiffly, she leaned forward, until she could lay her head against the pillow.

"Close your eyes. Relax." *In other words, don't watch me drool over you,* he thought with little humor. He settled his hands on her shoulders again, finding them even more tense than a few minutes earlier. Involuntary little sounds filtered from her mouth as he attended her, making him wonder if she moaned during climax. Damn. He shouldn't think about it.

But how could he *not* think about it when his fingers itched to slide under the edge of her stockings and tease her

skin, when he wanted to tug the hem of her skirt higher and
see if her underwear matched the satin of her garter belt.

He trapped a groan of his own and tried to focus on her
back. How delicate it was, how slender. The scent of her
perfume drifted around and through him. She wasn't wearing a bra under her top, but a lacy sliplike thing. What was
it called? He couldn't remember, but he wanted to see it. He
wanted to pull the skimpy blouse over her head and feast his
eyes on the skin and silk beneath, slide the straps down,
cover her breasts with his hands . . . his mouth.

A new scent reached him—arousal. He let go of the effort to restrain his own, knowing she felt the same. Welcoming the heat and the swelling, he closed his eyes and
slowed his hands, letting his fingers glide over her shoulders to press against her collarbone, feeling her push herself into the pressure in unspoken invitation. Did he dare let
his fingers drift farther, touch the nipples he'd earlier
watched tighten enticingly? Could he pull her back against
him and let her feel the strength of his desire as he ran his
hands down the front of her body?

This was crazy. He'd been hired to protect her, not seduce her. Ignoring the ache in his loins, he concentrated only
on her shoulders. Her eyes opened for a few seconds, as if
she was about to say something, then they shut again, allowing her retreat.

Paige jerked upright as the jangle of the phone sliced into
the tense quiet. Pushing herself off the chair, she stood and
straightened her clothes as she listened to his end of the
conversation, deciding Lloyd was on the other end. Rye had
his back to her, but she saw him attempt to unobtrusively
adjust his jeans. She didn't know whether to crow or cower.

She glanced at the holstered gun cradled under his arm.
His strength scared her a little. His pure maleness was a
hundred times more potent than she'd ever attempted to
handle. He could crush her so easily. She was inordinately
pleased that he was attracted, especially given their adver-

sarial relationship, but knew she was a fool to think he'd risk letting down his guard.

Then there was the matter of the woman he had spoken to so tenderly on the phone. Who was she? And how did she fit into his life? Where would *she* fit? A brief fling in a moment out of time? What the other woman didn't know wouldn't hurt her?

No. Paige thought more of herself than that. Still, it might be interesting to see how far she could push him and what he'd do about it.

"Harry."

She blinked and looked at him, deciding it wasn't the first time he'd called her name.

"Talk to Lloyd. Tell him what you need."

She forced her legs to move. "Good afternoon, Lloyd. I hope you caught up on your rest."

"I did, thank you, miss."

She rattled off the brand and model printer she needed. Hesitantly she asked if he might be willing to pick up something casual for her to wear, a sweat suit or something.

"Of course, miss."

"I don't need much. I might be going home today, for all I know, so don't spend a fortune. As for sizes—"

"Unnecessary, miss. I'll be there within the hour."

"But—"

He hung up. Paige held the phone out and stared at it, then shook her head as she set it down. Rye came out of the bathroom as she did so, his hairline damp, as if he'd splashed his face with water.

"What side of the bed do you sleep on?" he asked.

She straightened, surprised. "Why?"

"Because I'm going to lie down until Lloyd gets here, and I don't want to sleep on your side."

"To be honest, I kind of roll around."

"Oh. Well—"

"But don't let that stop you," she rushed to assure him. Anything to get him out of sight for an hour and let her think clearly. "I don't mind."

"If you're sure?"

"Positive. Please. Be my guest."

He closed the door between the rooms halfway, enough so that she couldn't see what he was doing, but could hear. Boots falling to the floor, the shift of fabric as he slid under the comforter. Lord. Nothing like this had ever happened to her before. Why now, when she was at her most susceptible to temptation? Was she having a mid-life crisis at age twenty-eight?

She stretched out on the couch to think. Her eyes drifted shut. It took too much effort to open them.

The sound of a key being fitted into the lock brought her awake. Lloyd entered, his arms loaded with packages. He nodded at Paige as she yawned and stretched. An hour had passed.

"Warner's asleep," she whispered, taking a couple of the bags from his hands.

"No, I'm not." He emerged from the other room, tucking his shirt in.

"Pasta salad for Miss O'Halloran and a submarine sandwich for you, sir," Lloyd said as he placed two bags on the coffee table. "I'll put your dinners in the refrigerator. Pop them in the microwave for five minutes or so when you're ready."

"Pasta salad . . . my favorite!" Paige said. "How did you know?"

"He's a mind reader. Be careful what you think."

"He's joking, of course, miss. I hope the clothing is as much to your liking."

She dug into a bag and withdrew a cream cable-knit sweater that would fall mid-thigh, soft blue jeans and a teal T-shirt and matching leggings. Two simple white cotton-knit camisoles, saved from being merely undershirts by their skinny shoulder straps, tumbled out next. Further investigation yielded white sneakers, size nine, narrow, and three pairs of slouchy socks. Everything looked as if it would fit.

"I don't get it," she said. "How did you know my size?"

Rye grinned mutely at him, seemingly daring him to answer.

Lloyd's expression never changed. "I have an eye for such things."

"I'll say. Good taste, too," Paige said. "What's in the box?"

"Chocolate chip cookies, miss. Homemade. From Mrs. MacKenzie, sir."

Rye carefully set down the sandwich he'd been about to take a bite of. "She doesn't know—"

"Of course not, sir. She has been on a baking binge and forgot I can't eat chocolate. Let me see if I have her words correct...I believe she said something about domesticity being the pits."

Rye chuckled. "That's my Kani."

"Who's Kani?" Paige asked as she sprung the lid on her salad.

The phone rang. Rye snatched it up.

"Yeah?...Put him through. It's your dad," he said to Paige as he waited for the connection to be made. "Patrick, what's up?...Did they trash the place?...Do you want to bring the police in on it?...Keep me current. I'll let you talk to Paige."

"Dad?" She clutched the receiver with both hands.

"Somebody broke into your house, honey."

"Oh, God! My presents! Did they take the presents?"

"Well, it's kinda crazy. Not much seems to be disturbed. I came to add water to the Christmas tree stand like you asked. The door wasn't shut tight."

"Ask him if they took your address book," Rye said to her as he paced, thinking.

"I heard him," Patrick said. "Where do you keep it?"

"In my drop-leaf desk in the living room. Nothing was destroyed? Are the presents under the tree?"

"I count about fifteen."

"That's probably all of them. Can't you find my address book? It's around six inches square, sort of peach colored." She could hear him rustling papers.

"Don't see it."

"He says it's gone," she said to Rye.

"What about at work? Anything missing? A Rolodex, maybe."

"Tell Rye I'll call when I get back to the office."

Rye extended his hand. "Let me talk to him. Patrick, listen, if something's gone from her desk, question everyone about who might have had access today. Maintenance men, delivery people, anyone who's not employed by you. If you come up empty, have your security people start running traces on your newest employees and work backward. Call me anytime... She's fine here with me. I promise. Even if they've got her Rolodex and can get my address, they won't be able to track us... Let me know as soon as possible."

Rye hung up the phone and followed Paige's movements as she paced in front of the hearth. "Don't you have an alarm in your house?"

She fired a glare at him. "No."

"A woman alone, in a big city?" he pressed.

"It's a quiet neighborhood. I've never had any problems."

"It only takes once."

"Look, Mr. Secret Agent Man, I'm upset enough without you criticizing my home security—"

"Or lack thereof."

"Indeed." Ice formed around the word.

"I can't believe you don't have a system. They're so easy to install."

"They're expensive."

Rye frowned. "Expensive? A thousand dollars for peace of mind and safety? I'd say they're a bargain."

She gestured impatiently. "Of course you would. You think flying first class is a *necessity*."

"Well, now that you've seen me, you must understand why I need plenty of room."

"I'm not responsible for your gene pool, Warner. I just pay the bills. We spring for business class on international flights. If you want royal accommodations, you pay the difference."

"It wasn't like that before you took over as comptroller."

"What can I say? I run a tight ship. We haven't lost money since I took over, either."

"That's because you're a—"

"I used to design women's clothing."

Lloyd's firmly enunciated words drowned out whatever insulting tag Rye was going to apply to Paige. They both stared at him.

"What did you say?" Paige queried.

"I said I used to design women's clothing. That's why I could estimate your size easily."

Paige eyed him, noting the slightest show of tension and deciding their argument had made him uncomfortable. "I apologize, Lloyd. We always fight like this. It's just the first time face to face. It's harmless."

Rye snorted. "Oh, yeah. I know it always makes *my* day. I really look forward to our *conversations*."

Her gaze flickered to him as he swept up his notepad and stared at the words there. It struck Paige that she *had* enjoyed their discussions. In fact, the last few times she'd called him to request receipts for his expenses and more detailed information about his invoices, her heart had pumped loudly in anticipation. She had begun to enjoy hearing him say, "Oh, for God's sake, Harry," when she questioned a ten-dollar breakfast or a cab fare he couldn't confirm with a receipt.

She had forced him into a better accounting of his expenses, but, in truth, she didn't want him to get perfect at it—so she occasionally changed the rules.

Not that he didn't get even once in a while. There was the time he had submitted a bill in paragraph form instead of an itemized list, forcing her to unearth the charges from a field of words. She'd paid the bill with forty-nine separate checks, one for each item, forcing him to endorse each check separately and complete several bank deposit slips. The bank had called her about it, curious and annoyed, but he had returned to a more standard statement format the next time.

She always found fault with his bill, but she had never really questioned why, until now. She'd have to give it some thought tonight while she took her bubble bath.

Paige and Rye ate in silence as Lloyd called housekeeping to request clean towels, then busied himself straightening the rooms before unboxing Paige's printer and helping her set it up. She asked him if he could wait an hour or so until she finished the project she'd spent the morning working on and could print up a copy to send to the office.

"I'm at your disposal."

"If you'd like something to read, I have a couple of magazines—"

He held up a hand. "I just realized that I forgot something, miss. I'll return in an hour."

"Oh. Okay. I hate putting you out."

"Think nothing of it, miss."

She watched him exit the room, the door closing on a whisper behind him, before she returned to the computer.

"Was Lloyd telling the truth or was he just trying to distract us?" she asked Rye later as he hung up from his umpteenth phone call.

"The truth?" He continued to write, her interruption barely breaking his concentration.

"Did he design women's clothes?"

Rye looked up and grinned. "Again, I'll leave the telling to him. He's had a checkered career."

Paige leaned an elbow on the table and propped her chin on the heel of her hand, considering. "Why don't you just leave me here with him and go about your business? It's obvious that's what you need to do."

He tossed his pencil down, stretched and rolled his neck. "Because I made a promise to your father."

"I'm sure he's only concerned that I be safe."

"What's going on, Harry?"

"I'm just trying to make your life easier."

"I don't think so. I think you've figured out you could manage Lloyd."

"I could?"

"He likes you, that's obvious. There's no way I'm leaving you with someone you can wrap around your little finger. You'd have him out sight-seeing by tomorrow. We can't take that chance."

"I wouldn't—"

"Like hell you wouldn't."

She frowned. "Well, maybe I would. But I'd be really, really careful."

"There's no such thing in this situation."

Paige pushed herself out of the chair and moved to the refrigerator. She pulled out two bottles of spring water, held one up to Rye in question, then passed it to him and opened her own. "I can't believe I got myself into this mess. It seems so... so like a B movie."

"Even his name's a cliché," Rye commented. "Joey Falcon."

The same thought had occurred to her more than once, but she bristled at his rubbing it in. "That's interesting. That was my impression of you at the airport."

"What was?"

"That you were a walking cliché, with your black leather jacket and everything."

"Black is unobtrusive. Am I supposed to wear camouflage?"

"Well, no, but—"

"You seemed pretty interested in me, cliché or no."

"I was not."

"You weren't checking out every inch of me by the baggage carousel?"

His self-assuredness irritated her enough to circumvent any embarrassment at having been caught surveying him. "I noticed you because I recognized you from the plane. And because you stood motionless when everyone else was working the kinks out after the flight. And because you seemed so fascinated with the woman in the red minidress."

"Sunglasses make great decoy devices. Believe me, my eyes were on you."

"The whole time?"

He stood and moved beside her as she warmed her back by the fire. Leaning an elbow on the mantel, he caught and held her gaze. "You were worried about the bags Lloyd had taken from you—enough that you kept a very close eye on them. You scanned me once, decided I was beneath your consideration, then continued your perusal of the area. But you couldn't help checking me out again, much more thoroughly. You hated not carrying anything out to the car, and you were very nervous following Lloyd away from the terminal to an isolated location. Does that about cover it?"

She took a sip from the bottle, stalling. "Okay," she said finally, "you're good at your job. Except that I didn't dismiss you because you were beneath me."

"Why, then?"

"Because I knew your ego would be proportionate to your chest size."

"Oh? Does my chest interest you?"

"Cut it out, Warner. Quit twisting my words."

"Well, you seemed not to mind it so much last night—or the rest of me, either."

She took another quick swallow. "I was *surprised* at your chest."

His voice registered more than mild interest in her comment. "Why?"

"I thought bodybuilders shaved their chests. You... don't."

"I don't compete, Harry. I pump iron to keep fit for my work. What do you do to keep so fit?"

She was flattered that he thought she looked good. "Dance aerobics, occasionally. I walk quite a bit."

"I would think you would need more than that, if only to blow off steam after work." He studied her. "I could have Kani put a program together for you, if you want. Yeah, that's good. That would give her something to do, too. She's going nuts waiting for the baby to be born."

"Who's Kani?" she asked for the second time that day.

The phone rang. "Yeah?" Rye said abruptly into the receiver. "Anything else?... Are you sure?... Hang on, let me ask Paige something." He tilted the receiver down. "Your Rolodex is gone. Do you have a duplicate anywhere?"

"I've got a short list in my laptop, but the complete business files are in my office computer. Some of my personal numbers are here with me. Why?"

"We may need to contact your closest friends, and it would also be a good idea to run off a complete list of your business contacts and have them faxed here. We can go over them together, decide if it's information we could use."

"All right. My secretary can retrieve the files, but it means having to reveal my password."

"This is critical. You can assign another password when you get home. Patrick, is her secretary still there?... Matthew?" His brows lifted. "Put him on for Paige."

He passed the phone to her. "A male secretary, huh? And you think *I'm* a cliché?"

She grabbed the receiver and tucked it between her ear and shoulder as she typed in a command to retrieve her address files from her laptop. "Matt? Yeah, hi. Are you at my desk?... I'll give you a list of names for my father, then we'll open the computer and you can run off a business list." She reeled off the personal contacts Patrick should be aware of, all the while trying to figure out how to give Matt her password without Rye hearing it. Suddenly, he disappeared into the bathroom and she took advantage of his absence to tell her secretary the password. "Barbarian.... Yes, as in Conan.... You might do well to remember that your review comes up in three weeks, Matt." She listened to him chuckle before guiding him into her address program, then asked for her father and handed the phone back to Rye at his request when he returned.

"Use the fax number I just gave you any time. The machine will be checked a couple of times a day.... Don't worry about her, Patrick. She's just fine here. Completely safe."

Rye hung up the phone, but left his hand curved over the receiver a moment as he debated with himself. Trying to let only mild curiosity come through in his voice, he said, "Your password is barbarian?"

Five

Her cheeks flushed with color. Instantly, brilliantly. Unwilling fascination ran a road rally through him. She was becoming three-dimensional to him, and he didn't want that. Not at all. The more elusive she was, the better he could protect her. The less interested he was, the more clearly he could function. *Barbarian?* She had used her nickname for him as her secret code to her most confidential information. *Why? And are you forgetting that you did something similar?* he reminded himself.

The front door opened behind him. Lloyd unwittingly saved Paige from answering and Rye from further contemplation. She hurried to her computer and punched some keys to start her work printing, then left the room. Lloyd passed a small bag to Rye.

"What's this?" He unrolled the top and peered in.

The answering voice was hushed and gravelly, reaching only Rye's ears. "Because you're charged to protect her."

"I don't need this." He shoved the bag against Lloyd's stomach.

"I've never known you to lie to yourself," Lloyd said simply, ignoring the bag.

Rye crushed the sack between both hands. "If I *can't* do anything, I *won't*. Don't put temptation in my lap."

"Temptation just strolled into the bedroom. If you don't take it, I'll give it to *her*."

"Blackmail, Lloyd? She's gotten under your skin that fast?"

"I believe the point is that she's gotten under yours, sir."

"So we're back to sir, are we?" He leaned into his friend. "I'll keep the gift, but I won't need it."

"Words, sir."

"So's no."

Rye noted his smile, grim but accepting. Lloyd had lived a long time, had seen a lot of things. He touched Rye's arm lightly, then moved to stare at the churning printer, leaving Rye to contemplate his gift-that-was-a-commandment—a dozen condoms.

He came instantly awake, snatching up the gun and swinging his legs off the couch in one fluid movement. On silent feet, he approached the front door and waited, listening, his eyes focusing briefly on the digital clock. Two thirty-five.

"Let me *go*."

The words were Paige's, the tone more like that of a lioness protecting a cub, half fear, half warning. She was dreaming, he decided. No one could have gotten past him, and the bedroom windows were impassable. Still, he didn't lower his weapon as he inched the bedroom door open.

A soft red glow from the hearth offered enough light to distinguish a fitfully moving mound in the bed. Unintelligible noises came from within. He set his gun on the nightstand and said her name quietly.

She went deathly still.

"Paige. Wake up."

Her breathing accelerated, almost to the point of hyper-ventilation. He hadn't wanted to touch her, had wanted to pull her out with just words, but his words weren't register-ing. He curved his hands over her shoulders.

"Rye!" she screamed, trying to jerk herself out of his grasp.

"I'm here, Harry. You're all right. Shhh. Shhh."

Her eyes flew open. Relief replaced fear, and she startled him by burrowing against his chest, her hands gripping his back, her fingers digging into his flesh.

Hesitantly, he let his own arms encircle her, touching her lightly, holding her loosely, then with a silent groan he hunched his shoulders and gathered her to him, tucking her head under his chin. He brushed a hand down her braid and along her back, feeling sweat-soaked fabric, before stop-ping at her waist to pull her more snugly to him.

"You all right?" he asked after a minute.

She nodded.

"Bad dream?"

Again, a silent nod, followed by quiet words. "I couldn't find you. I needed you, and I couldn't find you."

"I'm here. I'm not going anywhere." It took a Hercu-lean effort to still the thudding of his heart. She had needed him. She had *admitted* to needing him. And when she'd been in trouble, she'd called him Rye. Not Warner. Not Barbarian. Rye.

Her teeth chattered, chills from the damp pajamas and the letdown of fear.

"Would you like a drink of water?" he asked, knowing he had to break contact with her, break the temptation of her dependency.

"Yes, thank you."

He released her reluctantly; her hands dragged along him as well as he backed away, also unwilling to let go of the contact. He brought her a glass of cool water, then stoked up the embers and added a log.

He sat on the edge of the bed, facing her, and pulled the half-empty glass from her unyielding grasp to set it on the table. With the more radiant light from the fire he could see she wore pink flannel pajamas that threatened to arouse him more than a silk negligee on any other woman ever had. "Better?"

She nodded.

"Do you want to talk about the dream?"

She shrugged, embarrassment beginning to settle in. "Standard nightmare stuff. I was being chased and couldn't get away. Every time I rounded a corner, another man stood there, an evil grin on his face."

"Anybody you know?"

"Faceless, except for the grin." She shuddered. "It was awful. I felt so helpless." She rubbed her face with her hands, avoiding his gaze. "I'm sorry I woke you."

"I wasn't sleeping well anyway," he said, realizing how much he liked the softer Paige. With her hair braided but tousled and her designer clothes exchanged for pajamas, she seemed approachable and . . . well, *pretty,* for lack of a better description. She wasn't beautiful, not in that model-stunning sense of the word. But she had good bone structure and fine, distinct features. She would age well, staying pretty all her life. There was an elegance to her, almost a nobility in posture and manner that not only caught the eye but held it. Her lithe form seemed designed for exactly the kind of clothes she'd worn on the airplane, draped, soft and classy.

But he wanted to see her in a skin-hugging leotard and tights working out beside him at his gym, her chest rising and falling as she cooled down from an aerobics class, sweat glistening on her pale skin.

He watched her slide open the drawer of the night table and pull out a tiny box. The scent of chocolate filled the room, making his mouth water as she dumped two truffles from the box into her hand and offered him one. He accepted with thanks, and they didn't speak again until the candy was gone.

"Airline chocolates," he said. "You put them in your briefcase."

"I guess you *do* notice everything."

He smiled. "I was impressed with your self-control. Chocolate's a weakness of mine."

"Mine, too. I test myself."

"Why?"

"To see how long I can hold out."

"Why?" he pressed.

"I don't know. I just always have."

"Don't you ever just let loose? Break a few rules? Take some risks?"

She licked a speck of chocolate off her fingertip then raised her knees and rested her arms on them. "Not really."

He was curious about why she kept such tight control over herself, why she hadn't asked her father about her mother. Why she'd fallen so quickly for Joey Falcon, breaking an apparent lifelong pattern of analysis and self-control. Okay, he was more than curious about Falcon and what it was that had attracted her to him. He could even admit to a little jealousy.

He noticed she focused on his gun as she wrapped her hand around the almost empty glass of water beside her. Picking up the weapon, he pulled out the clip and ejected the round from the chamber. He held it out to her. "Nine-millimeter semiautomatic Beretta."

Paige stared at it for an instant. She let go of the glass and wiped her hands along the comforter before reaching for the gun. She attributed her shivering to the iciness of the metal, but it warmed instantly and she still didn't stop shaking. She let it lay in one hand and brushed the surface with her fingertips, up the handle, along the barrel. "How do you load it?" she asked, determined to conquer her physical reaction to the weapon.

He silently showed her the sequence.

"And to unload it?"

He walked her through the process and let her practice several times. "Have you studied any form of self-defense?" he asked.

Paige let the clip drop to the bed as he had instructed, then ejected the round from the chamber. Her finger off the trigger, she aimed at a still life painting above the fireplace, satisfied with how quickly she'd achieved competence in the technique. "Nothing extensive. I wouldn't ever own a gun."

Rye curved a hand over hers to snap on the safety, cautioning her to always handle the weapon as if loaded. "I'm not talking about owning a weapon, but learning to protect yourself. Given that Patrick has always feared you'd be a target, you've had good reason to learn. Why haven't you?"

She lined up a realistic-looking apple in her sights. "He's mostly bluff. I don't believe I've ever really been in danger. Not until this time, anyway."

"But you've had bodyguards before."

"Games," she said succinctly before making the sound a four-year-old makes while shooting a toy gun. "Applesauce," she drawled, then blew make-believe smoke from the tip of the barrel.

Rye's chest rumbled with quiet laughter. He accepted the gun from her and returned it to the table. "What do you mean by games?"

"Patrick the matchmaker. He was trying to find me a husband." She enjoyed Rye's reaction, a combination of shock and amusement.

"Are you in need of one?"

"Certainly not one my father would pick."

He eyed her for a minute, looking as if he wanted details, but when she offered none, he asked if she could sleep now.

She shrugged. "If not, I'll do some work."

"I'll say good-night, then."

Paige shed the bravado she'd wrapped herself in and closed her eyes as he left the room, shoving aside the fact that he'd seen her scared, not in control, *dependent*. He probably liked it, she decided, so that now he had something new to taunt her with. And yet, he had seemed accepting of her weakness, at least for the moment.

She wasn't. She hated that he'd witnessed it.

Her eyes opened as the sound of his voice drifted into the room, not words but a low timbre of sound punctuated by a few seconds of silence, followed by his voice again. He was having a conversation, undoubtedly on the telephone. She glanced at the clock. Two-fifty. Almost six, Boston time. Could he be calling her father? Telling him about her nightmare?

No! She had to stop him. It was bad enough *he'd* seen her helpless. Patrick couldn't know how frightened she'd actually been or he'd never stop treating her like a child.

She threw back the comforter, rocketed out of bed and had taken several steps when a tap sounded lightly on the door before being eased open.

"Who were you talking to?" she demanded.

His hand on the knob, Rye stared as she stood silhouetted before the fire. The flannel was opaque until it was spotlighted from behind, outlining her shape—the lean torso, smooth curve of waist and womanly swell of hip. He flipped on a switch, spilling light over her so that her body once more hid behind fabric.

Big mistake. Now a vivid picture of her was seared into his mind. Her sleep-mussed hair, makeup-free face and rumpled, soft pajamas made her seem too accessible, too normal. Too appealing.

"If that was my father you were reporting to—"

"It wasn't. Get dressed," he ordered, cutting off not only her words but his mental imaginings.

Her eyes blinked wide. "Why?"

"We're going out."

"Now? At three in the morning?"

"I can't take you out during the day, can I? Do you want to go out or not?"

"Give me ten minutes."

"Five. Don't worry about your hair. Just throw some clothes on. You won't be in public."

"Where are we going?" she called as he retreated to the bathroom and she opened the closet door to grab her jeans and sweater.

His answer was the sound of water running. Intentional, no doubt, she thought with some humor. He wanted either to surprise her or catch her off guard to see her reaction. *So let him,* she admonished herself. *I don't like surprises.* Yes, you do. *How do you know? No one's ever surprised you before.* You'd never met Rye Warner before.

Ah.

Grinning, she peeled off her pajama top and slipped into the cotton camisole that Lloyd had chosen, then shoved her arms into the heavy sweater. The jeans fit remarkably well, perhaps a little too snugly, but the length was good. The pristine sneakers were already laced; she tied them efficiently. By the time she was dressed, the bathroom was vacant. She rebraided her hair quickly, splashed water on her face, brushed her teeth and hurried into the living room. Seven and a half minutes, according to her calculations. Not bad.

Rye looked her over as he shrugged into his jacket. She was beaming at him as if he was some kind of savior. Maybe this was another mistake. Too late now, though. The arrangements were made, and he wouldn't disappoint her.

"Where's your coat?" he asked as he dug into his suitcase, hunting for the black watchman's cap he knew was there.

"I'll get it." She hurried into the bedroom and emerged sliding into a winter white wool coat with a neck-warming collar. The hem brushed her calves. From her pockets she produced woollen gloves. As she pulled those on, he settled the stretchy knit cap on her head, tugging it over her ears.

"We've got a half hour walk ahead of us, most of it hilly. Can you make it?" he asked.

"I can make anything."

"Are you claustrophobic, Harry?"

"Antsy."

He cocked his head at her. "You give the impression of serenity."

"Yeah, well, I'm a hell of a bluffer."

He stared at her a few seconds longer, wondering what else she was good at bluffing. Who was the real Paige O'Halloran? And did he really want to discover her?

"Stay to my left at all times," he said as he opened the front door.

"Okay."

Okay? No argument? No why? What was going on here? Was she really that desperate to get out of the cottage?

Questions, questions. He wouldn't ask her, wouldn't give her a chance to become any more human, any more vulnerable than she had already become. It had only been a dream, but in her dream she had needed him. In real life, she wouldn't. So he was safe. From her dependency, anyway.

She drew in a deep, cleansing breath as they began climbing the first hill. "God, that feels wonderful! Crisp and fresh," she said, her eyes adjusting to the darkness after the bright light of the cottage.

"Perfumed with exhaust."

"Don't be a spoilsport, Warner. I'm enjoying my freedom."

"You've been incarcerated all of thirty hours. Don't you think you're overreacting just a little?"

"It's not just being confined that's gotten to me. It's the *idea* of the whole thing. The fact that I *can't* go out." The fact I can't escape *you,* she added mentally. If absence was supposed to make the heart grow fonder, why was proximity doing it? She was finding him more magnetic by the minute. She liked his changing moods and attitudes, liked being caught off guard by the intense scrutiny he sometimes subjected her to. And she really liked the way his gaze skimmed her all over, with interest and heat, as if he was on death row and she was his last conjugal visit.

What would his skin feel like? Whenever she got within a foot of him, she felt him radiate heat. They wouldn't freeze in a snowstorm.

Stop it, Paige. He's being paid to do a job, so don't put too much stock into his actions. He's careful and he's a born watcher. *And* he may be taken already.

She freed her mind of unaskable questions and hiked silently beside him. She wished she'd taken a minute to stretch her leg muscles, because now they complained of being pushed after too much inactivity. Concentrating instead on her surroundings, she ignored the increasing tightness in her calves going uphill and the fiery burn in her shins going down. She glanced at him surreptitiously, noting he wasn't even breathing hard. She would have been gasping if her pride hadn't interfered.

Just about the time she had decided to swallow her dignity and ask him to stop for a minute, he pointed to a building.

"In there."

"The police station?"

He grinned. "Can I pick 'em or what?"

"Do I look like a cheap date? I expected dinner at least."

"The vending machines here..." He kissed his fingertips. "*C'est magnifique.*"

Paige laughed as he pulled the door open for her. The desk sergeant was classic—late fifties, white-haired and balding, a face that advertised he couldn't be shocked by anything. To her surprise, the men hugged briefly before slapping each other on the back.

"How's life been treatin' you, boy?" the officer asked after a curious look in Paige's direction.

"Not too shabby. How're Aggie and the kids?"

"Good. Real good. Got me a new grandbaby just last week. That makes six."

"All set for retirement?"

"Three months from tomorrow. I'm lookin' forward to the career change. Thanks for includin' me. This is the young lady you called about?"

Paige moved forward at her cue and extended her hand, but let Rye make the introductions. This was a man he trusted, she decided, when Rye gave him her whole name.

The officer, Mack, passed Rye a set of keys and a piece of paper. "Here's the security code, son. Cap'n says you can keep the keys."

"Thanks." Rye stared at the paper, then slid it into a pocket, along with the keys.

"One more block," Rye said to Paige as he held the door open for her to exit.

Intensely curious but determined not to ask him where they were going, Paige walked beside him. "How do you know Mack?" she asked.

"He went to the academy with my father, a long, long time ago."

"Your father's a cop?"

"He was. He was killed in the line of duty when I was nineteen."

"Oh, Rye. I'm sorry. How awful for you."

"Yeah, it was hard. The captain Mack referred to was my dad's partner at the time he was shot."

"Is that why you didn't become a police officer yourself?" She couldn't see his expression. She wished she could.

"Not really. I had an aptitude for broader investigation work, and I wanted to travel. I was lucky enough to have found a mentor who was willing to guide me until I was ready to be on my own. Here we are."

Rye let them into a small, plain building that had no sign on the front to indicate the name or kind of business. She followed him down a sterile corridor and into a glass-partitioned anteroom that looked out at a second room, where acoustical tiles lined the walls and ceiling. A pistol range.

"I'm going to shoot?" she asked, surprise flooding her. "Why?"

"You were going stir-crazy locked up with me, and I can't very well take you anywhere during the day. It was the only thing I could think of. Plus, I think you should know how."

"What's your connection to this place?"

"I designed the security. It's privately owned by four officers. Should be open for business next week. Mack will manage it full-time when he retires."

As he slid out of his jacket and hung it on a hook, Rye watched her move into the range and observe the empty room. Her anticipation was palpable. Adrenaline would take over for a while at first, limiting her skill until she calmed down. He'd lost the memory of firing a gun for the first time because he kept his skills honed with constant practice, although most of what he did involved using his mind, not his body. Martial arts training had been enough for his needs so that he rarely packed a weapon, especially since carrying a concealed firearm involved various permits for different states. It was another reason he'd insisted on Paige being sent to San Francisco, where he did have a concealed weapons permit.

"Hand me your coat, Harry. I'll hang it up."

Paige hunched her shoulders and let the coat slide down her arms, catching it before it fell to the floor and passing it to him. She tried to slow her heartbeat as she watched him draw his gun out of the holster, then pull out two clips of ammunition from his jacket pocket.

She didn't know why she was so fascinated with learning to shoot, a skill that had never even entered her mind before tonight. A gun represented power, although a power that could easily be misused.

Rye clipped a cardboard target to wire cables and pushed a button to send it twenty-five yards away. She hung on his every word, followed every movement of his hands and body as he explained what she needed to know. The world could have crumbled around them and she wouldn't have paid attention, she was so intent on learning the process.

After almost ten minutes of lecture on gun safety as well as instruction, he ripped open a small plastic bag and withdrew a two-foot string with a foam pellet attached to each end. "We'll wear double ears. Squeeze each foam piece down tight and insert it in your ear, then we'll add the earmuffs over them." He passed her a pair of muffs that looked like stereo headsets.

"Are you ready to try?" he asked.

Within the cushioning of the ears, Paige could hear her own breathing as if in a wind tunnel. She nodded. "No." Her voice sounded tinny and far away.

He grinned at the contradiction. "Your head says yes, your mouth says no, Harry. That's the sort of thing that gets women into a whole lot of trouble."

"I'm sorry. I've never done anything like this."

"Do you want me to fire first?"

She wanted that very much and said so. They both slid safety glasses on.

It was over almost before it began. She lost count of the shots at ten, but they were followed by several more. The floor was littered with shells that had hit the wall beside him and ricocheted down. The acrid smell of gunpowder filled the air, fading quickly. He brought the target close. There wasn't a shot outside the bull's-eye.

"I'm supposed to follow that demonstration?" she asked.

"I was a novice once, too, you know."

She shook her head. "Never. You were born with a gun in your hand."

"Are you done stalling, Paige? Your turn."

She watched him send the target into position. "Aren't you going to put a new target on so we know which ones are mine?"

He laughed. Loudly.

She settled her hands on her hips. "Well, I *might* hit one in the middle."

His brows lifted.

The gauntlet had been thrown down.

Imitating him, she rammed a clip in and switched the safety off. Concentrating on what he'd told her, she kept her thumbs forward and out of the way of the slide, pushed her right hand tightly into her left and focused on the sights. She wanted to be good at this. Good from the very first shot. Good enough to earn his respect.

She lined the sight with the bottom of the bull's-eye, then squeezed the trigger slowly, slowly, slowly, just as he'd instructed. Her heart stopped beating. No breath echoed in her head. She forgot about him. She forgot about everything except the target twenty-five yards away and the powerful weapon in her hand that wouldn't stop bouncing.

An hour must have passed before the gun fired and she drew breath again. "Wow," she said, soft and amazed. There hadn't been any noticeable kickback, although she had expected some, but the sound was loud, even behind double ears.

"This shot will come faster, remember," he said, keeping his hand on the weapon to keep it pointed away as she calmed.

"Wait a minute. Where did my shot hit?"

"Lower left corner. See it?"

"Oh." Damn. Not good. Not good at all. She had something to prove here. She had to do much better than that. She sighted the gun again, but her wrists wobbled and she couldn't hold the gun still.

"Anticipation," he said as she set the gun down for a minute. "It does crazy things to your mind, then travels down your arms."

"I wanted to be good at this," she muttered honestly.

"You've fired once and you expect perfection? Come on, Harry. Lighten up. Give yourself some time to learn."

"I'm not good at learning. I just like to do it—competently."

He resisted patting her shoulder, like a parent to a child. "That doesn't surprise me. But you're putting pressure on yourself that doesn't need to be there. Relax."

She picked up the gun again and sighted it. Beside her, Rye didn't move, but watched her jaw clench and her brow crease as she focused. He wanted to put his arms around her, wrap his hands over hers to help her keep the gun still. Liar. He wanted to have her in his arms again, needing him for... something. No, he didn't. He wanted her independent and strong and—

Boom!

"Where'd it end up this time?" she asked, her whole body leaning into the counter at hip level as she set the gun down.

"The edge of the bull's-eye."

She squinted at the target. "Really? Was I just lucky?"

"Maybe. Keep trying and find out."

She tossed a grin his way. "*Now* will you put a fresh target on?"

He showed her how to clean the gun after a half hour of shooting had worn her out. Her shoulder ached a little, but pride bubbled out of her at how well she'd done for a first lesson. As they walked back to the hotel, she glanced in Rye's direction, caught his indulgent smile and curved her hand over his upper arm. "I wonder what it would be like to be so strong."

"If that's something you're really interested in, you could build your strength substantially. You have to be willing to invest a little time and effort."

"How many hours a week do you put in?"

"Not many. Once you reach a certain level, maintaining it doesn't take that much effort."

"That woman you mentioned yesterday... Kani? Is she an employee?" She looked at him, trying to keep the hopeful expression out of her eyes. *Please say yes.*

He seemed about to answer her when he suddenly sent his gaze on a quick reconnaissance of the predawn surroundings. Paige held her breath as she tried to see whatever had put him on alert. The street was lit only by an occasional overhead lamp and infrequent car headlights, enough light to see while walking, but little enough if someone wanted to hide and attack.

She watched as he seemed to look at her but actually used the moment to look behind them. She wanted to turn around, to see what he was seeing. She settled for looking at him.

"Take my hand. Slow down," he whispered as he slid his gun out, keeping his hand inside his jacket.

"Shouldn't we speed up?" she whispered back, welcoming the solidity of his hand closing around hers.

"I want to know who's back there. I can't see anyone."

"Then why—"

"I heard someone."

They turned a corner, and Rye propelled them into a dark doorway, pressing his back to the door, pulling her against him and encircling her within his arms. "We're lovers," he said. "Hold me, too."

Paige hesitated before putting her arms around him loosely, allowing him quick escape, if necessary. He cupped her head to his chest with one hand, pressed the small of her back with the other arm, leaving his hand free to grip the gun.

She heard a person cough, then nothing but traffic, but even that was muted. Gradually, she became aware only of Rye, of the solidity of his chest where it pillowed her cheek, of his extraordinary warmth, of the sanctuary his arms made for her. Staying alert became difficult. She wanted to nuzzle. She wanted to fuse. She wanted. Period.

She felt his chin brush her hair, felt his hand slide slowly down her back, stopping at her waist to pull her snugly against him. Felt—oh! Felt *him*. His entire body seemed to get harder. His entire body.

She tipped her head back to look at him. His gaze never met hers; his words drifted above her. "I apologize. Don't take it personally."

Six

Don't take it personally? What does he mean, don't take it personally? He was hard, aroused. She was in his arms. She couldn't take that personally?

"He's almost here," he whispered as his hand made a slow sweep of her buttock, then stayed to massage. His hips moved against hers.

Paige fought panic. Half aroused, half furious, trying to listen for footsteps and trying not to react to his blatant masculinity pushed her beyond control. She squirmed, trying to get away. He held her tighter, shushed her into silence. She turned to stone as someone walked by, held herself rigid until Rye took his hands off her and pulled her out of the doorway to follow a block behind the stranger.

"We're okay," he said after a minute. "He's not a threat."

Paige didn't respond, just continued to match him stride for stride. She ignored him every time he spoke until he gave up altogether, although she sensed his bewilderment. As soon as they entered the cottage, she stalked directly into the bathroom, whipped off her sweater and washed her face and hands of gun oil residue and leftover emotion. She tried to calm herself. The adrenaline rush from learning to shoot had melded with the momentary threat of danger to make her edgy enough. But to add to the equation, her physical reaction to his touch and his subsequent dismissal of *his* reaction left her angry and humiliated—and wondering why he had the power to hurt her so much.

"Feel better?" he asked as she stormed into the bedroom.

Paige pressed her sweater against her chest, covering her camisole. He hadn't turned on the lights, but the fire had been stoked and now blazed with brilliance.

Rye stood slouched against the doorjamb between the rooms, his arms folded across his chest, one foot crossed over the other. When she merely shot a glare his way, he pushed. He didn't question why it was so important to him that she not lock herself up in chains of control. "You take offense quickly. I already apologized."

"If you're waiting for me to accept your apology, you might as well get comfortable. Mold's gonna grow on you before that happens. If I take offense, Warner, it's because you're offensive," she snapped as she flicked the comforter off the pillows, then yanked back the sheet.

He straightened and moved toward her. "It was an involuntary response—"

She laughed, a little hysterically. "Oh, I see. All cats are gray in the dark."

Rye stopped and analyzed her words, her voice, her body language. All of it indicated fury. He spoke hesitantly, feeling his way around her simmering emotions. "If you mean I would have responded to any woman the same way in the same situation, you're wrong."

"Oh?" Her voice was tight, her tone arch. "I was different in some way? But I'm not to take that *personally?*"

The light bulb clicked on in his head. She was embarrassed. She'd been attracted, too, but he'd squelched it with his poorly chosen words. He'd been amazed at his response to her with the potential danger hovering over them, but she had felt good in his arms. Perfect. Just tall enough, just curvy enough, just right.

He knew his reaction had been inappropriate for the moment and the situation they were in, and he'd been afraid she would be upset. Well, she was, wasn't she? *Work your way out of this one, pal,* he told himself.

"Maybe we need to acknowledge the attraction we're feeling, get it out in the open so we can deal with it," he said.

"I'm not attracted to you. That would be counterproductive, not to mention stupid. You're my bodyguard. We can't, either of us, become attached. If I was angry, it would imply emotional involvement. Which I don't have."

"I don't believe you."

"Tough."

Rye laughed. "Tough? That's the best you can do?" He'd been fascinated by her control, but her loss of control held him enthralled.

Paige glared at him, which made him laugh harder. "You are such a barbarian," she said.

"Well, this savage likes what he sees."

"That's not my problem." A little of the belligerence left her voice, replaced with uncertainty.

"No. No, I guess it's *my* problem." He stalked her. She stood her ground physically; emotionally she teetered.

"What are you doing?" she asked, distrust ringing in her voice.

"An experiment. You got mad at me for getting aroused when I had you in my arms—"

"That's not true." She hopped back as his hand shot out to grab her. "I was surprised at that, not mad. Don't touch me."

"Scared?" he goaded, dropping her arm then snatching her sweater from her and hurling it aside. His gaze focused on the plain cotton undershirt she wore, tantalizing in its simplicity.

"What are you doing?" She lunged for the sweater, but he restrained her with his hands against her shoulders. She jerked away from him.

"I just want to see what *your* involuntary responses are."

"What do you mean?" Suspicion spun a web around her words.

"Suppose, just suppose, mind you, that I were to take you in my arms again—"

"Don't touch me."

He held up open hands. "I won't touch. Use your imagination. I'll stay here, you stay there. Okay?" At her wary nod, he said, "Suppose I take you in my arms. Suppose I stroke your back like you did mine—"

"I did no such thing!"

"Didn't you?"

Paige looked around frantically, trying to recall the moment in the doorway. A vague image filtered through her mind of her hands reaching under his jacket to flatten against the solid warmth of him.

"Okay, maybe it was more like squeezing. Regardless, just suppose I rub circles over your back, slide my hands to curve slowly over your rear, lift you into me." His voice faded into a seductive hush, mesmerizing her. "Suppose I skim my hand around to brush your breasts. What kind of reaction—do you suppose—I might find?" He moved a step closer; his gaze shifted blatantly downward. "Maybe the kind of reaction you're having right now?"

Paige felt her nipples tighten until they poked at the soft cotton knit. The heat in his gaze intensified, amazing her. She was about as flat-chested as a woman could be. Consequently, she'd never felt particularly sexy. But she saw appreciation in his eyes that she wanted so much to believe was more than some kind of game he seemed to be playing with her.

She suddenly wanted him to put action to his words, craved his hands on her flesh. Instead, she curled her fingers into her palms and dug deeply for self-control. "Don't take it personally, Warner. They react to cold, too."

Rye smiled, then laughed. Then laughed harder. She didn't know how to respond.

"You are the most interesting woman I've met in a very long time," he said at last, a cockeyed grin on his face as he advanced on her. When the backs of her legs hit the bed, she scrambled up onto it. He followed. She kept retreating until she came up against the wall. "Now what? You're trapped."

"What do you want?" The words were forced from her throat.

He ensnared her with his arms against the wall. "This," he said softly as he dipped his head toward her, giving her time and space to get away or to stop him if she really wanted to.

Paige lifted her face and dared him with her eyes. The slightest smile of triumph flickered on his mouth as he brushed a finger across her lips, and she smelled a light fragrance of gun oil. They watched each other until the first gentle touch of lips and then her eyes fluttered closed as her body became a hard knot of need.

Oh, the taste of him! So hot and tempting. He deluged her with the most extraordinary sensations—kisses that started slow and teasing and built to strong and seducing. Lips that fit with hers perfectly, a tongue that both savored and enticed. She felt one large hand slip under her camisole and glide up her back, emerging from the top of the garment to feather her neck with caressing fingers, the fabric riding up her stomach, revealing a square of skin for his belt buckle to imprint its pattern against.

She dug at his shirt, yanking it out of his waistband so that she could spread her open hands against his back and explore the muscles and ridges and smooth, firm flesh. She drew her hands forward, traced the slope of chest, brushed her fingertips over his nipples...and wished he would do the same to her. The bunched fabric teased her with sensation as he moved against her—or was she moving against him?

All she knew for sure was that his mouth was expert at drawing her into oblivion and keeping her there. There was nothing but Rye. Rye...

"Am I doing that to you?" he asked against her forehead, leaning against her so that her back flattened against the wall.

"What?" She pressed her lips to his throat, clung to him with relentless strength as she tipped her pelvis up a little, trying to align herself with the ridge of denim that pressed her abdomen. Standing on tiptoe didn't help; she sank farther into the mattress, losing ground rather than gaining it.

"You're shaking."

Paige forced herself into stillness. She squeezed her eyes shut and took several deep breaths. "This is a mistake," she said.

"Maybe. But maybe it's just the wrong time and the wrong place." He stepped off the bed as she slumped against the wall. "Make no mistake, Harry. You're not a gray cat to me."

He had passed through the bedroom doorway when she smiled, a slow, lazy curve of lips. "Meow," she breathed, sure he couldn't hear.

He laughed.

Her cheeks hot with embarrassment, Paige changed into her pajamas with the speed of an Indy driver. He wasn't supposed to hear that. She hadn't said it loud enough to hear. But he had. Just as he'd heard her tell Matthew her password, even though a closed door had separated them and she had almost whispered.

Damn. She lay in bed, staring at the ceiling, contemplating the man. What new things had she learned about him in the last day and a half? Dogs didn't hear as well as he did.

He was an advertiser's dream as the "after" pictures for exercise equipment. He was big. Everywhere.

And he wasn't quite as interested in her as she was in him.

She folded her arms over her eyes, blocking the light from the fire. She had touched him a whole lot more than he had touched her. He hadn't even seemed tempted. She had run her hands all over his back and chest, hoping that he would explore her in return, but he hadn't. She had pulled as close to him as she could get, had waited for him to cup her rear and bring her even closer. He hadn't.

But he'd been aroused. That he couldn't hide.

She groaned and dropped her hands to her sides. Stop thinking about the physical stuff, she ordered herself. What else had she learned about him?

He was relentless about his duty, taking protective measures well beyond what was probably necessary for the situation. He was perceptive, having noted her interest in his gun, then actually doing something about it. He could be good company when he tried. His mouth tasted like heaven....

There seemed to be a woman in his life, and a child. And if that was true, she had no respect for him, because it would mean he'd taken advantage of her attraction to him.

She couldn't wait another minute to know. She was afraid of her reaction to him, afraid she would let him break barriers she'd let no other man anywhere near—and she couldn't allow that to happen only because she hungered for him. Pushing aside the comforter, she climbed out of bed and padded into the living room.

"What's wrong?" he asked instantly, the sound of shifting fabric indicating he'd probably pushed up on his elbows.

She knelt beside the couch and entwined her fingers in her lap. "Who's Kani?"

"My sister. Why?"

A tidal wave of relief flooded her so that she almost couldn't speak. She swallowed several times, fighting escaping emotion that was both unwanted and unfamiliar. "Is she pregnant?"

"Yes. She's due any day."

Her throat burned as she closed her eyes, grateful for the darkness that masked her reaction. "Was it Kani you talked with this morning, asking how the little one was?"

"Yes. What's going on, Paige? Why do you sound so..."

"So... what?"

"Small."

What a curious word, she thought. And yet it said so much. Her voice was layered with an insecurity he couldn't have heard before, but she knew all too well. "That's all I wanted to know," she said, starting to stand.

He curved a hand around her arm to stay her. "Why won't you tell me what's bothering you?"

"I couldn't sleep, that's all. Between the trip to the pistol range and what happened—" *in the bedroom* "—afterward, I'm just wound up."

"I'm sorry you were frightened by the man following us. There's no reason to suspect anyone could find us, but I won't take chances."

He'd misunderstood, but that was all right, she decided. "How do you live like that all the time? Isn't it exhausting never letting your guard down?"

"It's second nature by now. Stay alert. Stay aware. Stay alive."

"What's that? The Big Boy Scout motto?"

Rye laughed, although his mind wandered to the package Lloyd had given him. *Be prepared.*

Lloyd was on his mind too much tonight. Because he didn't want Lloyd proved right, Rye had controlled himself in the bedroom earlier, not giving in to the need to touch her as she had touched him. He had always been able to control his sexual urges. It was a sign of maturity. She should be no different. Control, that's all. It was a matter of control.

"I didn't thank you for taking me out tonight. I really did appreciate it," she said.

He shook his head. "I hear that hopeful tone in your voice, Harry."

"Well, what if I disguised myself some way? You know, I could have Lloyd pick up something to bleach my hair blond, and I would look totally different."

"I don't think that would be enough to do it. You'd probably have to change your appearance more dramatically than that."

"Like what? I'm willing to do anything."

He contemplated her body in his mind's eye, deciding what made her distinctive. "You could stuff your bra maybe, or—"

"Go to hell."

Idiot, he chastised himself as he clamped his hands on her to keep her from running off. His eyes had adjusted to the level of light and he could see her well.

"Come on, Harry. You know what I'm saying. A disguise has to make you appear different."

"And since I have no breasts at all, big ones would make me unnoticeable? I don't think so, Warner. I think it would draw attention."

"Well, they wouldn't have to be melon-size."

"As opposed to apricots?"

He almost laughed. She was embarrassed, affronted and generally ticked off. "So, you've got almost more nipple than breast. So what? Who cares? Aren't you comfortable with who you are?"

She got right in his face. "I'm so comfortable I don't even own a bra. So how could I stuff one?" She pulled away from him and stood, an avenging angel bent on proving a point. "You're just another muscle-bound jock chauvinist. I know your kind. You like your women busty and available. And you're bent out of shape because I'm neither."

He smiled benignly. "I don't care about your breasts."

"Right."

"I don't."

"Then why are you making such a big deal about it?"

"Them," he corrected. "Plural, not singular."

She scowled at him, almost breathed smoke through her nose and ears.

"And I wasn't making a big deal about them. You were," he said in a completely conversational tone.

"All men care about breasts."

"I'm not all men. And where do you get off presuming what I like or don't like?" He pushed himself off the couch, finally out of patience with her. "I like women as individuals. Sure, I'm attracted initially to a body or face, but in the end it's her personality that holds the attraction for me— and the way she feels about herself."

"I find that very hard to believe."

"Why? Oh, I see. Because I pump iron, I can't be sensitive to a woman."

"Maybe." Fascinated, Paige watched him prowl the room. With the rise of his anger came the ebb of hers. He shoved his fingers through his hair, stopped, stared at the floor, stared at the ceiling, then blew out a long, slow breath.

His voice was velvet over steel. "The sexiest woman I've ever known had only one breast the first time I made love to her and neither breast the last time I made love to her."

Paige went utterly still. She didn't take her eyes off him.

"She knew that her sexuality wasn't tied to her breasts. She knew that her sexuality came from here," he said softly as his fingertips pressed Paige's forehead before curling into a fist he placed over her heart. "And here."

"You cared for her very much," Paige said, wanting to draw him to her, wanting to comfort.

"Until death." The words seemed to knot in his throat and unravel on a rasp.

Her own throat felt tight and hot. She closed her eyes against the image of his pain as he slid his hands over her breasts, tenderly, nonsexually, as if he was touching *her,* his lost love, not the warm, living woman who recognized how painful it was for him to relive such tragedy.

The quiet tick-tick-tick of the mantel clock echoed into the silence like a grandfather clock to an insomniac. Called back, Paige focused on Rye. His gaze shifted to her mouth.

"Don't confuse me with her," Paige said quietly. An arctic chill sent shivers through her when his hands dropped away. The warm blanket had been comforting and life-assuring.

"No, I don't confuse you," he said as he placed a hand alongside her face, welcoming the silk of her skin against his. *You're strong; she wasn't. She was needful; you aren't. She tempted me with vulnerability; you don't.*

"I'm sorry," she said. "That she died. That you had to go through that." She rested a hand on his chest. "I'll leave you alone. Good night, Rye."

Rye. Funny how his name could sound like a caress, he thought, as he watched her disappear into the bedroom and the door close halfway. Now, how long before sleep would come?

He slept until Lloyd arrived, breakfast in hand. Groggy, he stared at his watch until the image focused. Seven-thirty—which meant he'd gotten a whopping five and a half hours of sleep, in two separate shifts. Someday soon he was going to sleep for eighteen hours straight and catch up. Maybe after this job was over he'd go to Hawaii for a week and vegetate on the beach. Recharge his batteries.

Lloyd's presence went almost unnoticed. Only a dim corner of Rye's mind concentrated on what his friend was doing—on the sound of a glass carafe being filled with water, of coffee being scooped and dumped into a paper filter, the solid clunk of mugs being set on the table. An olfactory alarm clock of bacon and coffee announced morning's arrival.

Paige wandered out of the bedroom, stretching as she walked. She hadn't changed from those damned pink pajamas that made her look like she was headed for a slumber party, except that she would have needed bunny slippers to complete the ensemble *and* there was nothing girlish about her. Why does a woman who wears incredibly sexy lingerie wear such plain fare to bed? And why was the sight of her in it sexier than any negligee?

His unwilling gaze followed the sway of her hips as she headed toward Lloyd.

"Good morning," she said, shuffling up beside him to stare at the breakfast he was laying out on the table—bacon, scrambled eggs, grapefruit and English muffins. "Oh, yum. This looks great."

He cast a quick glance her way. "May I get you a robe, miss?"

She waved a dismissive hand. "Why? He's already seen it all."

Rye held up both hands in innocence as Lloyd turned his head in Rye's direction. "What she means is that I've seen her in her pajamas already."

And was barely even affected by it, Paige thought as she finally looked at him. At least she'd gotten answers to her questions about the enigma of Kani and her impending offspring. That was a relief. Although the revelation of his past love had raised new questions she had no right to ask.

"Did you sleep all right?" she asked Rye as he joined her at the table.

He shrugged. Lloyd appeared with a robe, which he held for her to slip into. Paige grinned at him; his placid expression never wavered.

"Thank you, Lloyd."

"No sense your getting chilled, miss."

"There was hardly any danger of that with the fire you've got blazing," Rye remarked as he bit into a piece of bacon.

"Fires can flare up and cool down quickly," Lloyd said cryptically.

Paige eyed one man then the other, wondering at the exchange of expressions. Lloyd seemed to be admonishing Rye for something, and Rye seemed to understand clearly what he meant.

"We went on a date last night," Paige said into the heavy silence.

"A date, miss?"

"Uh-huh. First, we went to San Francisco's finest."

"Finest what, miss?"

"Finest. As in police."

"I beg your pardon? Did you have some kind of trouble, sir?"

"Don't call me sir. We went to the pistol range so that Harry could learn how to handle a gun."

"Excellent idea, sir."

The coffee had stopped brewing, and he poured cups for Rye and Paige. "How did you do, miss?"

"It was an adventure," she answered with a grin.

"Was it?"

"I had a great time, especially because I did very well, for a first time, according to my teacher. It was a thrill."

"Firing a weapon was thrilling, miss? I don't understand."

"Not firing it, but learning how. It was...spontaneous, and enormously satisfying. Like...like—"

"A quickie," Rye inserted, a wicked grin on his face. "I'll have to remember that in the future. If I take a woman shooting first, I won't have to spring for dinner."

"You know, Warner, I had you pegged for a romantic," Paige said with blatant sarcasm.

The phone rang. Instantly all business, Rye moved quickly to answer it. Paige concentrated on finishing her breakfast, but she could tell from his conversation that her father was on the other end and that the news wasn't good.

"I want to talk to whoever you brought in on your end, Patrick.... Because too many people are getting involved here. You can't put everyone into protective custody.... Look, do you know where Falcon's family is? Parents, siblings, anybody...? Because there's a good chance he'll contact them over Christmas, right?"

Christmas. I have to be home for Christmas, Paige thought, as she walked to the window, pulled the curtain back and looked out. There wouldn't be even a possibility of snow in San Francisco.

"You're wrong, Patrick. If they're out of state, that's even better. He'd feel safer going there.... Just give me the name and number of your security guy.... Woman? Who?... Where'd you find her—in the Yellow Pages?... Because I know all the good ones, and I've never heard of her.... Okay, okay. She can call me. But I want to hear from her today. Hang on. Paige wants to talk to you."

"Dad? What's going on?"

"Someone's been contacting your friends, hunting for information. Fortunately, no one knew where you were."

"I don't want my friends in danger because of me. Who got called? I need to talk to them and explain."

"No, you won't. It will jeopardize everything," Rye said as he made some notes on his yellow legal pad.

"But—"

"It's being handled, kid," Patrick said.

"I am fed up with both of you treating me like a child. This is *my* life that's in danger, and *my* friends who might get caught in the cross fire. Don't tell me I can't do anything. I need to do something." She glared at Rye and sent the verbal equivalent to her father over the phone lines.

"Convince your bodyguard, not me," Patrick said.

Her voice softened considerably. "Dad?"

"What, honey?"

"Tomorrow's Christmas eve."

"I know. I know."

"I have to be home."

"It may not be possible this year."

She closed her eyes against a rush of emotion. "Is it snowing?"

"Don't do this to yourself, Paige. Your mother—"

"Christmas is all I have left of her. It's all I remember. And that it snowed."

"But it's been so long, honey."

"You can't tell me it doesn't bother you. I've seen your face. Some years I've heard you—" She glanced at Rye, who seemed to understand her need for privacy. He gathered up some clean clothes and went into the bathroom, immediately turning on the shower. Lloyd took the dirty dishes out to the car.

"Sometimes on Christmas eve I heard you crying," she said to her father, who had remained silent, awaiting her. "And swearing. And throwing things across your bedroom."

"But she was my whole life."

"And she gave me mine. Somehow, some way, I have to be home."

"We'll do the best we can. That's all I can promise. You're obviously being tracked. Until we resolve this, you'll have to stay where you're safe."

"But why not closer to home? And why does Warner have to be the one to watch me? We could arrange something that would work just fine back there."

"This is *my* decision," he said so forcefully that Paige sat back in surprise. "If you and Rye don't get along, that's too bad. He's the best. You know it. I know it. I wouldn't entrust your life to anyone else. No one. Do you understand that?"

"Yes, sir." The words were not uttered like a concession, but an automatic response to an order, soldier to officer.

"*Are* you getting along with him?"

"Adequately."

"Meaning what?"

"Meaning...meaning nothing." Except that he confuses the hell out of me, she thought.

Silence, then, "Are you falling for him?"

"Of course not!"

"Paige?"

The shower water cut off, and she knew she couldn't say any more because he would hear her. "Everything's fine."

"It wouldn't be smart to get involved with him."

"Involved?"

"Personally. You know what I mean."

"Why not?"

"Because he's not like you."

That caught her attention. "Meaning what?"

"He's very, well, passionate."

"And I'm not?" Fury laced each succinct syllable.

"I don't think I can explain it to you, honey."

"Try."

"He's just...Rye's just different. He'd overwhelm you."

The hair dryer came on. "I can't believe we're having this conversation," she said, but forged on anyway. "Maybe I would overwhelm him. Did you ever think of that? And how do you know he's so passionate?"

"I just do."

An image flashed in Paige's head of Rye wearing only his briefs, holding her, kissing her, peeling her clothes off her and caressing each spot as it was uncovered. Would she stay passive through that? *Could* she?

She wanted to find out.

Lloyd came back in and looked surprised that she was still on the phone. "Shall I—"

She shook her head. "Call me later, Dad. Keep us informed of everything, okay?"

"Watch yourself, kid."

Paige cradled the receiver then pulled her knees up to sit cross-legged on the couch. The morning had been ruined. Her friends were at risk, her father was ignoring her ability to think logically, Rye was invading her thoughts *and* affecting her libido way too much. She had to find some way to end this business and get back to her routine, where she could find her center of calm again, not be wondering why he wasn't interested in pushing up her undershirt and tasting a nipple that openly begged for his touch. Her lack of control over her situation was taking a lot out of her. She was suddenly exhausted.

She'd never been particularly adaptable, so she'd always kept her life in balance, telling herself that she liked herself and her life just the way they were. She'd been honest in telling Rye she was comfortable enough with her body not to even own a bra; frankly, the way she looked hadn't mattered much to her. She'd concentrated her efforts on her actions, had tried to imitate the way she deduced her mother had been—elegant and calm, patient and gentle. All her life her father had told her how beautiful her mother had been, how she'd kept his temper under control, how quiet and self-assured she'd been. Paige tried to live up to the example set before her, and for the most part she felt she succeeded, although she often fought her own temper and impatience. She knew she was really more her father's daughter than her mother's.

But if her mother had lived? she mused. What then? Would I have been free to pursue my own interests rather than policing Dad? She'd never know the answer to that— her mother was gone, and her father would never change.

"May I get you anything, Miss O'Halloran?"

Paige filed away her introspection with a sigh. "Do you have children, Lloyd?"

"I have never had that pleasure, miss."

"I think you would be better at it than my father."

"From what I'm hearing, your father loves you very much. Is more necessary?"

Paige smiled at him, thoroughly chastened. "Thank you, Lloyd."

"For what, miss?"

"For reminding me of priorities. What about you? What are your priorities?"

"To help others. To appreciate the life I have. To serve Mr. Warner."

"Is that in sequence?"

"They intertwine."

"How did you meet him?"

"Why, he saved my life, of course."

Seven

"Shower's free," Rye announced as he made a timely entry into the room.

Paige ignored him. "How did he save your life?"

"He—"

Rye stopped behind her. "If you plan on taking as much time getting ready today as you did yesterday, Harry, I suggest you start now."

Paige tipped her head to look at him upside-down. "I checked my appointment calendar, Warner. It's empty."

"You can't take a hint, I guess. I'd like to speak to Lloyd alone, please."

She turned around to face him, kneeling backward on the sofa, and he was struck with a need to kiss her good morning, as if it would make the difference between his having a good day or a bad one. If Lloyd hadn't been there—

"You said you'd let Lloyd tell the story," Paige reminded him. "Have you changed your mind?"

"I'm not stopping him from telling it to you. I really do need to talk to him in private. Please."

She gathered her robe around her and muttered as she walked away. "I'll bet he's conveniently gone when I'm done."

"Did you say something, Harry?"

"You heard me perfectly well, St. Bernard ears."

The door closed none too quietly behind her, and he grinned. "She has a sassy mouth, doesn't she?" *And sweet, and hot, and demanding,* he remembered with tempting clarity.

"I don't like the look on your face," Lloyd said.

"I wasn't aware there was one."

"Don't hurt her. Just promise me you won't hurt her."

Rye crossed his arms over his chest. "Exactly what are you saying, old friend?"

"I'm saying that you've got a lot more experience in short-term relationships than she does. She's not a woman to take lightly."

"And exactly how do you know that?"

"Because I see past the desire in her eyes. I see through to the innocence. You should, too."

"She's a woman of the nineties," Rye scoffed, recalling the way her hands had explored him and deciding she was no innocent.

"I'm telling you, she's not like any other woman you've known."

Rye scooped up his pad of paper and flipped through pages without seeing anything. "And I've told you she's safe with me. Hell, she practically threw herself at me last night. I didn't take advantage then, and I won't now." He lifted his gaze abruptly, as if to punctuate the proclamation with a physical exclamation point.

Lloyd bowed tightly.

"Now," Rye said, "are you really going to tell her the story of how we met?"

"Why not, sir?"

He sighed dramatically. "Quit acting like my butler. I interrupted your telling of the tale because I wanted to make sure you told her the straight story, not the embellished one you created for my sister."

"Mrs. MacKenzie is a performer. She admired my recreation."

"And you relished her reaction. But to my knowledge you've never told another soul. Are you sure about this? You hardly know Paige."

"I know enough. She won't think less of me."

"Well, just to make sure my part is portrayed accurately—how many other men were involved?"

"Six, sir."

"How many?"

Lloyd's head bobbed in concession. "Three."

"And their weapon of choice was?"

"A huge, menacing—"

Rye lifted his brows.

"Pocketknife, sir."

"Exactly. Remember that. Why don't you sit down for a minute while I check my messages. I've got a list of things for you to do today."

Rye hung up the phone after a few minutes and stared at his notes. "Interesting. A man left a message saying Patrick O'Halloran referred him to me and would I please call him back about a job."

"I gather you don't believe it."

"Patrick's like a parent who's found the perfect babysitter. He doesn't give out my name to anyone." He dialed the phone as he spoke. "Did you notice how faded Paige's voice became when she spoke to her father about Christmas?"

"Yes, sir."

"Any ideas on why?"

"Something to do with her mother, I gathered."

"She died when Paige was four, she said." He announced his name to Patrick's secretary then continued his conversation. "I'm bothered by the lack of action in Boston. His investigators aren't uncovering anything useful."

"You believe you should go yourself?"

"She wants to be home for Christmas. If I take her back and set her up somewhere safe, I could get on it personally."

"Her father doesn't want her there."

"Yeah, well, he's not the expert, is he? Hello, Patrick?"

"What's wrong?" Patrick asked quickly.

"Did you refer a Carl Smith to me?"

"Hell, no."

"I didn't think so. Okay, we've got a lead. Take down this number and have your people check into it." He quoted the phone number and added specific instructions on how it should be handled. "I won't call this guy back until one o'clock our time, but I'll call you first. I also want to talk to your investigator."

"I've put a call in to her. She'll be here. Anything else?"

Rye picked up his pen and doodled concentric circles on the paper. "I want to know why Christmas is so important to Paige."

"Ask her."

"Why won't you tell me?"

"You're living in each other's pockets, Rye. It'll be a great conversation starter when you can't think of anything to say."

"Will it make her sad?" *Will it make her need me?* he wanted to ask. She had to be strong. He needed her to be strong.

A long stretch of silence preceded Patrick's response. "Does that matter to you?"

The round doodle turned plaid with bold vertical and horizontal lines. "This is tough enough on her. I don't want to add to it."

"It's probably not a good idea for you to get too personally involved with each other."

"Meaning, I shouldn't ask?" Rye heard deafening silence before Patrick rushed through his next sentence.

"Sorry. I've got to take another call." Click.

Curious, Rye set the phone down. As much time as he'd spent with Patrick, and as well as he knew him, the man remained an enigma. He was a man of deep feeling; he was also a man of convenient tales. Patrick bent the truth enough that "blarney" should be his middle name. But he wouldn't take any chances with his only child, Rye reminded himself.

"You said something about a list, sir?" Lloyd prompted him quietly.

Rye flipped through pages until he found the one he wanted. Ripping it off with a flourish, he passed it to Lloyd, who stared at the list for several seconds. A smile came and went.

"Very good, sir."

"Can you get everything today?"

"Of course. Tell Miss O'Halloran I'll be back."

"She's gonna be ticked off that you're gone. She'll blame me."

"Indeed, sir."

Rye chuckled as Lloyd left. The shower had stopped a while ago, then the blow dryer had come on for a rather long time. What did she do that took her so damned long to get ready?

"I knew it!"

Rye looked up from his notes as she emerged half an hour later.

"He's gone." She stalked to the window and looked outside for Lloyd's car.

"He'll be back. The extra hour he saved not waiting for you meant he could get more done, and earlier." He sat back and admired the full roundness of her rear as she continued to stare out the window as if it would bring Lloyd back. She hadn't put her hair in her usual twist, but had braided it, making her seem more accessible, less like an accountant, and she was wearing the body-hugging leggings and long T-shirt Lloyd had chosen. Rye flashed on an image of himself coming up behind her and pressing his body to hers, an image so vivid he could feel her pushing back against him so that they touched all the way down, leaving his hands free to caress her. *I don't even own a bra,* she'd said. Which meant she now probably wore only the undershirt again. The skimpy undershirt that her nipples jutted against. She had brought fragrance into the room, and memories of last night. They melded in his loins and pounded unmercifully.

Paige turned around. "Why are you looking at me like that?" she asked, folding her arms under her breasts.

He casually dragged the pad of paper over his lap. "You look nice." Definitely no bra. Temptation sat on his shoulder and whispered to him to move. Duty landed on his other shoulder and spoke firmly at him, sounding very much like a certain old friend of his. He conceded the argument to Duty.

She touched her hair. "Thanks. Is that all? You look . . . weird."

He lowered his gaze to the paper he held. "I've just got a lot of work to do."

"Don't let me stop you."

"What are you going to do?"

"Well, since I have no work to do—and no one to pass the time with—I guess I'll watch television. But I'll watch in the bedroom so that you can work." She poured herself a cup of coffee, offered him one, then retreated.

He blew out the breath he'd been holding and picked up the phone.

"Talk shows, talk shows," Paige grumbled to herself, changing channels for the thousandth time since she'd ensconced herself in the bedroom. She'd begun creating topics of her own and periodically called one out to Rye. "Men who love baby food, and the women who puree it for them," she'd shouted the first time.

"Personal experience?" he queried back.

Then later, "Women who love their chauffeurs, and the men who drive them wild."

"Should I warn Lloyd?" he asked.

And later, "Women who like to sleep on the right side of the bed—"

"And the men who *left* them," he finished, appearing in the doorway and leaning against it. "Women who interrupt work, and the men who tolerate them."

She smiled, because he didn't look like he meant it. He looked, in fact, as tired as she felt. Lack of sleep. A layer of tension. It was taking its toll on them both. He rolled his head one way then the other. "Come sit down," she said, patting the bed and moving back so that he could sit on the edge.

She swung to her knees behind him and pressed her fingers into his shoulders.

"Ah," he groaned, as she kneaded his spine from neck to waist. He shifted his torso and closed his eyes as she manipulated his shoulders, working the joints, loosening knots of tension.

"Where'd you learn this?" he asked.

"Twenty years of playing piano and ten years of working with computers have strengthened my hands. I took a class in massage." As he turned to look at her in surprise, she pushed his shoulder forward. She worked in silence for several minutes before starting to scratch his back instead, watching with satisfaction as the tiny hairs on his neck rose.

Rye hunched forward when her fingers shimmied just below his shoulder blades. Her hands zigzagged up and across his shoulders. "What is your perfume called?"

"My father took me to Paris when I graduated from high school. I had it blended especially for me."

"Ah. No wonder I couldn't put a name to it."

"Is that important to you? Never mind, don't answer that. You need to identify everything." She rested her hands against his back. "You look exhausted. Why don't you lie down here for a while. I'll go out on the sofa."

"There's room for two," he said quietly.

"Don't tempt me." *How's that for honesty?* she asked him silently.

Rye waited a couple of seconds before turning around. "I'm trying not to. How about in return you don't hang your underwear out to dry on the shower rod."

She squeezed her hands together and resituated herself to sit cross-legged. "I only expected to be here a couple of days. I'm sorry if it's in your way."

Rye pictured the midnight-blue satin garter belt and matching bikini underwear, and the bridal-white silk and lace garter belt and unbride-like panties draped like a lingerie display in the bathroom. His gaze drifted down her body, stopping at the juncture of her legs. "So what color are today's?"

"Peach," she managed to answer.

Peach. "You're such a contradiction."

"Am I?"

"Prim and proper outside. Sizzling underneath."

"S-sizzling?"

"I wonder..."

"You wonder what?"

"If you taste like a peach, too."

He nudged her feet apart and moved closer, lowering his head slowly, again offering her the chance to say no or to pull away. When his lips touched the sensitive spot below her ear, she closed her eyes, tipped her head back and let her body react to the touch of his mouth as it brushed her in a feathering caress. His tongue trailed the neckline of her T-shirt as his hand settled at her waist and crept upward. He drew a deep breath then released a sound she'd never heard before, a cross between animal and human, desire and control.

"Not peach," he breathed. "Paige."

She moaned at the way he made her name seem like a plea.

"Dammit."

Eight

—

His muttered curse accompanied sudden retreat. Confused, she watched him sit on the bed, lean against the headboard and draw a pillow into his lap.

"Lloyd's back," he said hoarsely. "Stretch out on your stomach or something. Like we've been watching television together."

Paige giggled. Her eyes grew large and round. "But Dad wasn't supposed to be home for *hours*," she whispered dramatically, a teenagerish lilt to her voice.

"Harry."

"He'll ground me, I just know it. And the prom is next week—"

"Shut...up."

She laughed harder, enjoying the flush on his face, a combination of passion and guilt. "What's the matter? Did Lloyd tell you to keep your hands off me?"

He fired a look at her that froze her laughter in her throat.

THE EDITOR'S "THANK YOU" FREE GIFTS INCLUDE:

▶ Four BRAND-NEW romance novels
▶ A Porcelain Trinket Box

PLACE FREE GIFT SEAL HERE

YES! I have placed my Editor's "thank you"
seal in the space provided above. Please send me 4 free
books and a Porcelain Trinket Box. I understand
I am under no obligation to purchase any books, as
explained on the back and on the opposite page.

225 CIS AWJP (U-SIL-D-09/95)

NAME

ADDRESS   APT.

CITY   STATE   ZIP

Thank you!

THE SILHOUETTE READER SERVICE™: HERE'S HOW IT WORKS

Accepting free books places you under no obligation to buy anything. You may keep the books and gift and return the shipping statement marked "cancel". If you do not cancel, about a month later we will send you 6 additional novels, and bill you just $2.66 each plus 25¢ delivery and applicable sales tax, if any.* That's the complete price, and—compared to cover prices of $3.25 each—quite a bargain! You may cancel at any time, but if you choose to continue, every month we'll send you 6 more books, which you may either purchase at the discount price...or return at our expense and cancel your subscription.

*Terms and prices subject to change without notice. Sales tax applicable in N.Y.

"He did?" She turned her head at the sound of the front door opening. "I have a champion?" *Do I want one?*

"We're in the bedroom," Rye called out.

Lloyd appeared in the doorway, his arms laden with packages, the most important one wafting with the scent of pepperoni.

Paige sprang up. "Pizza! How do you know all my favorite foods?" She snatched the box from his arms, planted a quick kiss on his cheek and headed to the living room. By the time Rye joined them, she'd grabbed three sodas and a mound of napkins and piled everything on the table in front of the sofa. She sat cross-legged on the floor and encouraged a balky Lloyd to join them, but he refused, saying he had several things to take care of. After stowing away the remaining packages, he left.

As he ate, Rye sifted through a pile of paperwork Lloyd had brought, then checked his watch. Time to call Patrick.

"What do you mean you haven't been able to trace it?" Rye demanded. "Put your investigator on."

"She's not here yet. She's working on getting the number."

"This is ridiculous. I'm bringing Paige back to Boston on the next flight. I'm taking over this circus." He ignored the hopeful look she gave him.

"There's no need for that. Wait a minute, here she is right now. Hang on."

"Patrick—" Rye realized he was talking to dead air. He'd been put on hold. "Your *father,*" he said, exasperated.

"You don't have to tell me. But he's just so darn lovable."

"Pigheaded."

"That, too."

Patrick came back on the line. "It's a cellular number."

"Great. Just great."

"I take it that isn't good news."

"We can easily find out who has the number, but we'd need a court-ordered warrant to track where it is now." Rye drummed his fingers on his thigh as he thought about the next step. "Well, I'll call him and see what comes of it. Let me talk to—"

"Sorry, Rye. Someone just came in. Let me know what happens." Click.

Rye dropped the receiver but caught it before it landed on the floor. He slammed it down. "I don't *believe* him. He is determined to keep me out of this investigation. He must be hot on the trail of something and won't share it, afraid I'll bring you home too soon."

Paige pushed herself up and got rid of the remains of their lunch. "Is there any chance of my being home for Christmas?"

"If I was there and in charge, you'd stand a better chance."

She sat beside him on the sofa, passing up a great opportunity to get after him about his lack of humility. "Let's grab a flight home right now. We can find a safe place there."

"It was risky enough having you fly out here. Every time you use public transportation, you run a further risk." He laid a hand over hers clenched tightly in her lap. "I can threaten your father all I want. In the end, he knows and I know you can't go home until this is resolved, whatever that means. I'm sorry. I know Christmas has some particular importance for you. I wish I could change things."

"The weather channel says it's going to snow."

Rye turned to watch her. "It's just a date on the calendar, Harry. You can celebrate it December twenty-eighth just as easily."

She tensed beside him but otherwise gave no indication of her feelings.

"Shall I give the mysterious Carl Smith a call?" he asked, suddenly needing to change the subject.

"Sure."

"Rothchild's Imports," a woman answered after two rings.

"Rye Warner returning Carl Smith's call."

"He isn't available, Mr. Warner. Is there a number he could reach you?"

"I'm afraid not. Is there a better time to contact him?"

"I'm sure it would be easier to have Mr. Smith call you."

"I'll just try later." He hung up as the woman again requested that he leave a phone number.

He repeated the conversation to Paige, not getting a response beyond her nod of acknowledgment. "I don't know about you, but I could use an hour's rest," he said.

"Go ahead and stretch out on the bed. I'll sleep here."

At the bedroom door he turned. "Do you want to talk about your mother?"

"No."

He stared at her a moment longer, wondering what it was about her mother that was so private—and perversely grateful she didn't want to share. The last thing he needed was for her to start confiding in him.

The overhead light came on, startling her awake. Disoriented, Paige struggled to establish time and place when Rye's voice gave her the answers.

"It's two a.m., sleepyhead." Something landed on the bed. "Get dressed in these. We're going out on the town."

The door closed behind him. Paige pushed herself up and blinked at the fabric strewn across the comforter. She and Rye had spent the remainder of the day and evening with him making phone calls and her flicking the remote control on the television, never stopping long enough to get into any story. Lloyd had come and gone, not staying to talk, muttering something about a homeless shelter and meals to be served.

With thumbs and forefingers, she lifted the clothing in front of her—a sky-blue leotard and white tights. Where does one go at two in the morning wearing exercise clothes? Deciding she didn't care—it mattered only that he wanted to surprise her again—she threw off the covers and hurriedly changed, adding her jeans, sweater and coat. She met him at the front door in a record six minutes.

Forty minutes of walking the hills of San Francisco found them in front of the Good Health Club.

"I take it you know the owner," she said as he punched a code in the alarm panel and unlocked the door. She stayed in the shadows until he'd flipped on lights and closed the blinds over the windows.

"I know the owner personally," he said finally.

"You, I assume."

"There are four of us. I needed a place to work out during off hours. It seemed like a good solution."

"So, this is the beginning of my program, I believe you called it. Did you talk to your sister about me?"

"No. Don't worry, Harry. I can give you plenty to do."

"And if I don't want to?"

"I am in no way forcing you to do this. I provided the clothes so you could. It's your choice. You can sit down and wait or find a mat to curl up on and sleep. I need to do something. You're stuck waiting."

Paige considered the condition of her legs, which were still sore from last night's trek to the pistol range. Added to tonight's longer journey, she decided she'd need a crane in order to stand up tomorrow, but a workout appealed to her, too. "Is there a Jacuzzi to use after we're done?"

He grinned at her as he set the tension on a stationary bike. "You can take your pick, Harry. Jacuzzi or massage."

"Given by you?"

"Well, of course. C'mere. Try this out."

She stripped off her outer garments and climbed on the bike.

"Give it about ten or fifteen minutes," he said, "then we'll switch you to something else. Have you ever used weights?"

"Paperweights."

He smiled. "One in each hand?"

"More like a shot put competition after a fight with my father."

"Broken any windows?"

"Just fingernails."

Rye laughed. He watched her for a few seconds, questioned if the tension was all right, then he stripped down to exercise clothes and settled himself at the butterfly press.

"Have you been a bodyguard often?" she asked after ten minutes of trying to ignore him in his tank top and shorts, his muscles bulging more with each press of the machine.

"Only a few times—" *grunt* "—and never for a woman."

"What kinds of jobs do you do?"

"Nothing glamorous. Most of what I do is anticipating." The last word was dragged into syllables as he worked the machine hard.

"Meaning what?" She became suddenly fascinated with the sheen glowing from his skin.

"For example, when an executive is going overseas—" *grunt* "—especially into a hot spot, I'll fly there ahead of time, check out hotels, business locations, transportation, things like that—" *a long, excruciating groan* "—then I'll arrange for security people."

"You're an advance man?"

He stopped pressing and slumped a little, relaxing his muscles. "Specializing in antiterrorism for executives. Actually, I was sent ahead of *you* twice."

"Really? When? Where?"

"Lisbon and Hamburg. Before you took over as comptroller."

"Not exactly hot spots."

"No. But your father doesn't take chances. I also take on a lot of embezzlement cases, especially when the person has fled the country." He started another repetition; a few more minutes passed. "How're you doing?"

"Can legs scream? I think I hear mine."

He chuckled. "That bad? I guess that means we skip the stair-climbing machine." Her pursed lips were his answer. "Let's get you working with some weights."

Paige eased off the bicycle, ignoring the grin on his face as she moved gingerly his way, rubbing her rear as she walked. She accepted two chrome weights.

"They're only five pounds each. The trick is to curl them slowly and methodically. I'll stand facing you, using my own. You just copy the movements. Okay?"

"You Tarzan, me Jane."

"You don't have to do this, Harry. Just say no."

"I want to. I really do." She watched him slide some weights onto two dumbbells. "How much do those weigh?"

"Each weight is ten pounds."

The calculations were simple. "Sixty pounds? You lift sixty pounds with one arm? No wonder you carried me so easily."

"Hell, you're a feather. Okay, try this."

He watched her concentrate on imitating him, and he tried to ignore her body, which was about as close to naked as someone could get and still be completely covered. The leotard clung to her. In the mirror behind her, he could watch her buttocks tighten, the thong cut of the leotard leaving her flesh covered only by stretchy white tights. The fact that Lloyd had chosen the garments when he'd charged Rye with protecting her gave him pause. Lloyd had to have known what watching her work out in the clingy stuff would do to him.

He changed the motion and she mirrored him, focusing on his arms. He fixated on her breasts, on the way the tips had drawn tight with the strain of exercise. The scent of her had stayed with him all afternoon, a new perfume he'd permanently cataloged. Now, a light film of perspiration made her skin gleam, and her cheeks flushed pink from effort. She looked tantalizingly beautiful, and Temptation sneaked in to sit on his shoulder again. Duty made an immediate landing on the other.

Diverting himself, he set his dumbbells aside and told her to lie down on the weight bench. When she did, he straddled the bench over her abdomen and showed her how to use the weights from that position. Her distinctive scents rose to swirl around him, luring him relentlessly. He wanted her. All of her. Temptation urged him on.

Paige eyed him warily when he snatched the weights from her and set them aside. "What's going on?"

He pulled her up so that she also stood straddling the bench. He watched her make a quick scan of his body, her eyes widening as she saw what he took no pains to stop from happening. He desired her.

"I need to know if you feel as good as you look," he said, sliding his hands around her waist and down over her rear. Duty yelled in his ear.

"Shut up."

Paige blinked in surprise. "I didn't say anything."

"I know," he murmured as he lowered his head. When their lips touched, he was filled with her—with her scent, with her flesh, with her answering need.

Paige wrapped her arms around him and pulled herself closer. She had no idea what had brought on this sudden mood of his, but she wasn't about to fight it. His hands kneaded her buttocks, then lifted her higher against him as she opened her mouth a little more to let his tongue make rhythmic forays against hers. The breath he exhaled heated her skin, and the hungering sounds flamed her body. A low, deep throbbing resounded through her as their mouths fought for position and awareness fled.

He dropped onto the bench, pulling her down to lie on him, never breaking contact with their mouths. Without having to support her, he could touch her as he'd wanted to. Temptation cheered. Duty hollered disapproval.

"To hell with Duty," he said, low and hungry, as he brushed kisses along her shoulder.

"What?"

Her voice seemed a million miles away to him.

"I want to see you. Feel you. Taste you." He felt her pull up a little and he opened his eyes. Her own were heavy with arousal; the scent of her wrapped him in need.

"What's changed?" she asked, unable to believe that he could lose control with her after keeping it so well before.

"Every time I close my eyes I see you as you were last night, wearing that damned undershirt, your nipples hard and begging. I need to know what they taste like."

Paige sucked in a quick breath at his words, held it as he pushed her up to sit tall. His fingers snagged the straps of her leotard.

"May I?"

"Yes," she breathed. "Please, yes."

He peeled the fabric down and off her arms, revealing small, perfect breasts with hard, dusky nipples. She moaned and closed her eyes as his hands covered her flesh with radiant heat, then a thumb and forefinger measured each taut peak, defining size and texture.

"Rye," she breathed, his name a long sigh of need.

He did a fast sit-up, cupped her rear with his hands. Standing, he carried her to the butterfly press. Seating himself so that he could lean against the upright cushion, he settled her in his lap, urged her to wrap her legs around him, then he bent his head and tasted her.

"Rye!" No longer a sigh, but a plea. She curved her arms up the back of his head as she arched her neck, giving him access. He tugged her hips closer, until she felt the hard length of him cradled at the spot she felt swollen and achy. He drew one nipple into his mouth, then the other. He laved her flesh with his tongue and nipped her lightly. Steam rose from the heat and sweat. She pulled his shirt over his head, and they rubbed slickly against each other.

Her throat vibrated with sound as waves of sensation rolled through her, past clothing, past lifelong denial, on into the core of her womanhood. Just the pressure of him against her swollen need made her tight and taut and hungry for things unknown, for things suddenly necessary to her well-being. She shook with need, moaned as she pressed her open mouth to his again and again, then to his eyes, his temples, his cheeks, and back to his mouth as her arms locked around his neck.

Rye wanted to lean her against the nearest mirror and fill her with himself in one smooth stroke, to drive them both to mindless satisfaction, the walls of mirror reflecting their bodies connected and in motion, from every angle. He wanted to hear her cry out with pleasure, wanted to know he'd done that to her, wanted to lose consciousness in her.

A tiny sound escaped her as he pulled back, needing to slow it down a little, afraid of his own strength, afraid he would unwittingly hurt her. She loosened her death grip on him. Her hands drifted down his chest until her fingertips caught the waistband of his shorts. Their gazes locked.

"Can I . . . ?" Her voice was filled with an uncertainty he could only wonder at.

"God, yes."

Paige slid a hand beneath the fabric and encountered warm, smooth, hard flesh. She watched him close his eyes and grit his teeth, and a sense of power engulfed her, foreign in its satisfying strength. Emboldened now, she adjusted the shorts until she could see all of him, could hold him in her hands and stroke him. On some level she was aware of the throaty sounds he made and the movements of his hips, but mostly she focused on touching him, exploring the masculine heat of him, iron-hard and down-soft.

He wrapped a large, callused hand around her wrist, halting her explorations. Silently, he hooked a finger into the crotch of her leotard and pulled it aside, then shifted their positions until he could trap his pulsing hardness against her. He released his hold on the fabric, sheltering himself between her leotard and tights. She cupped the length of him and he covered her hand, guiding them toward a duet of impending explosion.

"I don't have any protection with me," he said quietly, hoarsely. "Do we need it?"

"I'm...I'm not on the Pill."

His jaw clenched. Paige leaned against the wall his arm made for her back. She slid her hand from where it clung to his neck to stroke his mouth with her thumb.

"Can't we do something?" she asked, squirming.

He seemed to struggle with some inner debate. Finally, he pushed his fingertips along her hand as it shrouded him. "Is this okay with you until we can get back to the cottage and do it right?"

Right? There was something wrong with this? she wondered. It got better? "This is fine," she whispered.

"Arch your back a little," he directed, bringing her hips tighter and leaving her breasts free to explore.

He took a turgid nipple into his mouth as he started their hands moving again. Uncounted seconds flew by, time lost to the world and not mourned for their passing. His hand tightened on hers, almost painfully, and a deep, deep pressure began to rumble within her. It built and built, was intensified by the potent sucking of his mouth on her tight flesh, until it dynamited exultation from her in a fury of sound and movement matched by his own glorying release, lasting beyond a measure of time. Echoes of fulfillment faded into deafening silence as they drooped against each other, streaming with sweat, struggling for air.

After a minute, Rye slid a hand between them, making necessary adjustments.

"That was better than chocolate," she said into the quiet, her mouth pressed against his collarbone.

"Just think what it'll be like later."

Raising her head took extreme effort, but she managed it. She looped her arms around his neck. "Do we need to find some all-night drugstore first?"

"No."

He didn't elaborate and Paige didn't question him further.

"The showers here don't comfortably fit two," he said. "Let's throw our clothes on and go back to the cottage. We can shower together first."

"There's only one problem. I can't move."

He laughed.

"I'm serious. I can't move my legs. They're dead. I may never walk again."

He scooped his hands under her rear and stood. She grunted as her legs fell to the floor, gasped as she tried to support herself, groaned when he let go of her to stand alone. She wobbled for a second, forced one leg forward, then the other, until she took several steps. He stayed close behind her, in case she needed him. When she looked up, she saw them reflected in the mirror.

I'd like a picture taken just like this, she thought suddenly. They were naked from the waist up, and their skin glowed from exercise and loving. She watched as he hooked his arm around her, pulling her to lean against him.

"You're so beautiful," he said softly. He slid a hand down to cover one breast. His thumb brushed a dusky crest. "Are you sore?"

"Who cares?"

He smiled. Carefully, he pulled up her leotard. Scooping her sweater off her neat stack of clothing, he dragged it over her head. He never took his eyes off her as she finished dressing and he put on his own clothes.

It was the darkest time of night and the moon only a sliver of light to guide them. Words seemed unnecessary to the moment, and yet Paige wondered if she should warn him. She debated for blocks as she enjoyed the feel of him while they walked arm in arm up and down hills. Contentment wove a thread around them, binding them together. Anticipation began snipping at it the closer they got to the cottage. He finally gave her an opening.

"What are you thinking about?" he asked.

"You. In bed. Under my control."

He groaned in good humor. "They say men have one-track minds. I deserve hazard pay just for being near you."

She closed her eyes briefly, gathered her courage, then spoke in a hurry, before she lost her nerve. "Enjoy the battle, Warner. How many times in a man's life does he get a cherry bomb dropped in his lap?"

"You're confusing munitions with fireworks. Even so, I have the feeling that any bomb *you* dropped could bring a nation to its knees."

"I'm only interested in doing that to one man. And it's a cherry bomb," she repeated emphatically, cryptically, watching him closely. "It needs your fuse before it can explode."

His smile left his face by degrees—in puzzlement, awareness, then disbelief. His arm dropped away from her; his steps slowed. "Are you saying— No."

She held her breath as he looked away from her, made some mental adjustment and looked back.

"How can that be, Paige? You're twenty-eight years old. My God, you went away to college. You must have dated, and—"

"Why doesn't matter. I just thought that maybe it was something you needed to know. Ahead of time. You know, so you can make it special for me. Like the books say."

His jaw dropped. "Hitting me with a two-by-four would have had less impact," he said finally.

They stopped talking as they reached the hotel, were silent until they entered the cottage. Rye flipped lights on and stoked the fire with unnecessary force as Paige stood awaiting him. Finally, he turned to her.

"Let me be very clear of your meaning. You're telling me that you've never had sex before."

"That's exactly what I'm telling you."

He slammed the mantel with his palm and swore, leaving Paige bewildered at his reaction. "You act like I've committed some crime against nature," she said.

"I didn't want this. I don't want this," he said to the fire.

She felt her cheeks burn in embarrassment and anger. "Let *me* be very clear of *your* reaction here. You're *mad* because I'm a virgin? You're *mad* because I haven't been with another man? *This is a bad thing?* I thought that was something all men wanted."

He swung around to face her, gesturing with outstretched arms the exasperation he felt. "I told you before, I'm not all men."

"Are you saying that you don't want me now?" Her voice sounded pitiful, even to herself, but she maintained perfect posture and a semblance of control that came from years of keeping it when all around her crumbled. "If that's what you're saying, tell me now. Don't make me beg."

Nine

Rye's biggest fear loomed like a specter before him. His weakness was vulnerable women, a fact he had finally acknowledged several years ago. He hadn't realized it in the beginning. First there had been Joanna, whom he'd held and soothed as the ravages of cancer and chemotherapy had stripped her of hope and dignity. He had needed to be with her. It hadn't mattered that he'd gotten little in return because his comfort had been knowing he'd made her final days bearable. That was all that had counted. Then had come Terri, his best friend's widow, who had found herself suddenly without a husband and who turned to Rye for comfort. And he'd given it, because she had been so in need, and he had so needed to give. When she had let go of him to move on with her life, he finally realized he had to avoid women who needed him, because he gave up too much of himself in the process.

Now there was Paige, who stood on a huge precipice of vulnerability. She'd never entrusted herself to a man before, and that's what making love came down to—absolute trust between a man and woman. No one forgets the first time. He would be charged with making it perfect for her. It was a responsibility he would never take lightly and would remember too well afterward.

He couldn't do that to her, and he wouldn't do it to himself. A bond would be forged between them, and she would think she needed him, when what she really needed was to stay strong and in control.

But to lie to her and tell her he didn't want her? It was a hell of a choice. In the end, he compromised. "I don't want the responsibility," he said and watched her react as if he'd hit her in the stomach. Her arms hugged her waist and her chin jerked upward.

She headed toward the bedroom, then spun around as she reached the door. "Tell me what's changed."

"I never would have done what we did if I'd known," he said, apology in his voice.

"Why?"

"Because you're right. Your first time should be something special, something memorable."

She stalked toward him. "You don't think *that* was memorable? I never realized it could happen like that."

"There are an infinite number of ways," he said quietly.

"I am fast becoming aware of that. Oh, I know enough from movies and books to know that it isn't man-on-top, woman-on-bottom all the time. And I know...outside stimulation can work, too. I *didn't* know it was equivalent to learning a trade, however. That I had to be some kind of journeyman in lovemaking to be good enough for your bed. *No apprentices allowed.* You should tattoo it on your... forehead."

He did his best not to react to her hurt. It seemed kinder to let her be angry. "You didn't act like any novice."

"Again I ask, is that a bad thing?"

"You said you were a good bluffer. I just didn't realize you were bluffing me."

"I *responded* to you. I haven't put on any kind of act. Unlike you." She moved to within inches of him and glared right in his face. "I'll tell you what. I'll go find myself a man to apprentice with, then I'll give you a call. We can make love and I'll critique and compare the two of you, so that you know what your own level of expertise is."

He frowned. "Expertise doesn't matter as much as enthusiasm—"

"Ah." Her expression was that of a conqueror. "And you should know. Expertise, indeed. 'Expert tease' is more like it. You don't want me. You never wanted me. It was a game for expert players and I'm just a novice. But I learn fast."

"Look," he thundered, suddenly out of patience, "I didn't ask for what happened tonight any more than you did. It complicates the hell out of the job I was hired to do, and I don't imagine it makes your life any easier, either. There are sights and sounds floating around my head and diving into my gut that I know no amount of batting down will eliminate. You're going to haunt me until my dying day. Is that what you want to hear, Harry?" He grabbed her hand and pressed it to the placket of his jeans. "Feel that? You think I don't want you? I've been standing here trying to breathe through my mouth because you smell like sex, the best kind of sex, earthy and endless and free of inhibition. I could toss you onto that bed in there and drive myself into you and stay there for an eternity.

"Not want you? I'm trying to do right by you." *And me.* He shoved her hand down and turned from her. "Go to bed."

"Like now I'm supposed to be able to sleep," she muttered as she complied with his order.

"Yeah, well, at least you'll be tossing in comfort," he called out.

Paige breezed into the bedroom, swept up her pajamas from the floor where she'd dropped them, then stormed into the living room. "Take the damned bed, Warner."

"I'm not—"

"I am sick and tired of your griping about it. You made the damned arrangements, not me. But you've acted like it's my fault you've had to scrunch up on the sofa while I've sprawled in luxury." She poked a finger at his chest. "Well, never let it be said Paige O'Halloran can't compromise. Go on. Enjoy."

An hour passed. Rye had listened to her shower away the scent of their lovemaking, flounce onto the sofa and toss and turn, as he had been doing in the bed that was too big without her. He rolled off the mattress and moved on silent feet into the living room to crouch beside her.

Her eyes were open. He thought a sheen of tears layered them, but it might be his imagination. "I'm sorry," he said quietly.

Paige threw herself at him, buried her face against his neck and locked her arms around him. "Me, too," she whispered.

"We're in an untenable position," he said, stroking her back.

"I know. This is all so frustrating to me. I'm so angry that I even got myself into this mess I could spit. I'm taking it out on you."

"Being locked up together hasn't helped." He pulled back to look at her. Making a decision, he swept her into his arms, carried her to the bedroom and deposited her on the bed. "I should be in the living room where I can hear more," he said as he released her.

She caught his wrists as he drifted back. "You're not mad at me anymore?"

He shook his head. "I was more mad at myself than you."

"Yeah, me, too."

As he got to the doorway she called his name and he turned.

"When this is all over," she said, "maybe we should talk about everything that's happened. I still want it to be you."

"You still want what to be me?"

"My first." *My only,* she realized with sudden agonizing clarity.

He looked as if he would ask a question, then changed his mind. "We'll talk," he said, then he was gone.

They woke to rain, torrents of it. The sound it made pelting the roof was normally music to Paige's ears. She loved the rain, loved being cozy by the fire while the watery sounds surrounded her house. Except today—because it was Christmas eve, and it was snowing in Boston.

She knew now she wouldn't make it home in time for Christmas. Phone calls back and forth with her father confirmed that the holidays were getting in the way of discovering information, or so he said. Calls to the elusive Carl Smith yielded only a recorded message of unavailability. Rye still believed Patrick was hiding something crucial, wanting to solve the crime himself and be a hero in his daughter's eyes. Do criminals take holidays? She guessed that some did. Too bad it had to be the ones out to get her.

Lloyd came and went, bringing food, passing along cryptic messages to Rye, something to do with the rain delaying his ability to provide what Rye had requested. Rye continued to work, on several different cases, he said, moving endless stacks of paperwork across the table in some form of organization only he could fathom.

Paige was bored—thoroughly, tediously, relentlessly bored. She fluffed pillows around her in bed, flipped through channels with the remote and used her laptop to chart why she should or shouldn't make another attempt to get close to him, all the while keeping an eye on the open door between them and a finger hovering over the Close command on her keyboard. Every time he glanced into her room, she gave him what she hoped was a come-hither look, and he just stared at her. After the third try, she gave up and searched for something else to do. She did have a certain amount of pride, after all.

Digging to the bottom of her cosmetic bag she found an old—probably several years old—bottle of nail polish. She held out her hands to inspect her fingernails. Useless. Too short and too ugly for polish. Besides, one of the reasons she'd stopped using polish was that she always peeled it off as she stared at the computer screen and pondered a problem. She stretched out her legs and wiggled her toes. A definite possibility, she thought, scrounging through her bag again until she dredged up a plastic bag stuffed with cotton balls.

She had just finished separating her toes with cotton and was applying the first coat of Moonrise Magenta—whatever had made her buy that outrageous color was beyond her powers of recall—when Rye strolled in and stopped beside her, watching her pull the brush carefully across the nail of her big toe.

"Do you always stick your tongue out when you concentrate?" he asked when she'd almost finished a second toe.

"Also when I kiss."

His mouth twitched, whether with humor or annoyance she couldn't tell. He sat beside her, and she frowned as the brush slid off her nail and onto the cuticle. Without fingernails or an orange stick, she couldn't fix the mess. She sighed as she capped the polish, giving up.

"Are you stopping?" He stared at the two painted and three unpainted toes on her right foot.

"I was just killing time."

He shifted until his back was propped against the pillows alongside her, his legs stretched out straight in imitation. She wiggled her toes; the cotton jarred loose and she leaned forward to adjust it so it wouldn't stick to the wet nails.

"How're your legs?" he asked.

She shrugged.

"Still sore?"

"I'll live."

"Glad to hear it."

"Your sarcasm is unwarranted," she said. "What do you want me to say? I'm in so much pain I can barely move?"

"So those *were* grimaces of pain you were sending me a while back. Why didn't you say something?"

Paige hooted. So much for her attempts at seduction.

"What's so funny?" he asked.

"Me. I'm funny. The pain is tolerable. Believe it or not, I was trying to send you 'let's get naked' looks."

His brows drew together. "I was distracted—"

She pinched his cheek and plastered a fake smile on her face. "You are so sweet."

"I thought we decided to ignore the attraction for now."

"We did. I'm just practicing. Gonna need to know how sometime with somebody, right?"

Paige caressed his face with her gaze. Now that she knew, she didn't know how she'd missed it. She was in love with him. She'd started loving him over the telephone, with his devastating logic, rapier wit and utter sense of the absurd. Now she'd fallen the rest of the way, hard.

If she thought it would do any good, she would crawl onto his lap, declare her love and seduce him unmercifully. It wouldn't do any good. He didn't want her love, much less her body. And all because she was a virgin. Who could figure that one out?

Rye cleared his throat and looked away from her steady gaze, then fixated on her feet. "Why did you quit painting your nails?"

"Frankly, because you sat on the bed and jostled my hand. I smeared the stuff, and I don't have anything to fix it with. Plus, I'm not good at it, anyway. The last time I polished my nails was about four years ago, I think."

He stared at her feet another minute. "You're really going to leave them like that?"

Paige looked at her toes, then at him and laughed. "Why does it bother you so much? Once they've dried, I'll put socks on so you won't be so distressed."

"I don't like things done halfway, I guess. Whatever. If you can stand it, I certainly can."

She wiggled her toes again; her gaze turned speculative. "You could finish the job."

He bumped the wall in surprise. "Me?"

"Sure, why not?" She tossed the bottle at him; he caught it on the fly.

"You don't think I will," he said, slapping it against his other palm.

"Or can," she challenged. "Without making a mess."

He told her to lie down and put her feet on a pillow in his lap. "I'm doing this," he said, "not because you challenged me—I don't have to prove anything to anyone—but because I can't stand a half-done job."

"Okay," she responded cheerfully.

He fixed her with a hard look. "It's the truth."

"I believe you." She grinned. "And guess what? I don't care what your reasons are. I'm just happy that you're doing it for me."

He struggled along for several minutes in silence. She wanted to close her eyes and simply enjoy the attention, but it was so much fun watching him concentrate on the unfamiliar task. He didn't quite stick his tongue out as he worked, but his jaw clenched and his eyes squinted.

"This stuff is goopy," he said.

"It's really, really old."

He glanced at her briefly. "You wouldn't have left this undone, would you?"

"Of course not. Like you, I finish what I start. But your purely masculine response intrigued me."

He made her switch sides of the bed, so that he didn't have to bridge the newly painted foot to get to the other one. "I'm a feminist, you know," he announced.

"He says proudly as he paints my toenails."

"I *am* proud of it. I've never subscribed to the theory that a woman, like land, was meant to be possessed. Women are equal to men in intelligence and ability. Not in physical strength, of course, but women are stronger in other ways."

"What ways?"

He finished the slow stroke across her toe before looking at her. "Emotionally. That's a word with a lot of individual meaning, I know, but it says it for me. You have tremendous emotional strength, Paige. No one would have faulted you for falling apart at some point during this experience, but you haven't. You've fought it." He concentrated on the next toe. "When my father died, I thought my mother would break into pieces. She stayed stronger than any of us. And you'd have to know my mother to understand how shocked I was at her ability to find peace in his death, especially when he died so suddenly and brutally."

Paige propped herself on her elbows. "What happened?"

"He was an undercover vice cop. A drug deal went bad— someone snitched. He was killed...violently. But my mother somehow accepted that it was part of his job, had always accepted that it was a possibility. She has great strength."

"Tell me about her."

Rye chuckled. "She's so different, so hard to describe. Kani calls her scatterbrained, but that's not quite right. She's almost childlike."

"In what way?"

"In her enthusiasm for life. Kani's the same way, except she has the power of logical thinking to help her. Mom is Tinkerbell. She just *believes,* in goodness, in loyalty, in the Golden Rule. She's amazing. Kani has the same kind of trust."

He put the final flourishing stroke of polish on her little toe then admired his handiwork. "There. What do you think?" He held both of her feet by the arches and lifted them for her to see.

She jackknifed up to inspect his efforts. "I'm impressed, Rye. Very impressed. Are you sure you've never done this before?"

He arched a brow at her, correctly interpreting her pretended amazement. "Lie still until they dry."

"Yes, sir. Thank you, sir. You are ever so kind, sir."

"Paige?"

"Hmm?"

"Shut up."

Lloyd showed up within the hour, bearing a dinner that smelled heavenly. Rye and Paige had tugged the sofa closer to the fire, propped their feet on the table, and were sipping a flavorful cabernet sauvignon when he arrived.

"Come join us." Paige waved to Lloyd.

"I need to get to the shelter—"

"It's Christmas eve. The fire's lovely. The wine's delightful. Enjoy it with us for a few minutes."

"Your dinner will grow cold."

"I *like* my food lukewarm."

Lloyd's mouth quirked into a rusty smile. "Very well, miss," he said as he seated himself beside her so that she was sandwiched between the men. "No wine for me, though. I'm a recovering alcoholic."

Paige balanced her glass against her thigh. "I'm sorry. I didn't know. Does this bother you?"

"Not at all, miss. I've been sober for seven years."

"Good for you. You must be very proud of yourself."

"I'm grateful to be alive. That's all."

She swirled the wine in the glass, decided she didn't want it any longer, then set it on the table. "What do you think of my hot pink toenails?"

"Very shocking, miss."

She wiggled them. "They are, aren't they? I rather like them, though."

"Indeed. Quite lovely, actually."

"Rye painted them," she said, glancing at the silent man beside her, wondering at his thoughts. He looked utterly relaxed, yet she knew he could spring into action in a millisecond.

"He is a man of many talents, miss."

"Including saving lives, you said. I'm ready to hear about that, if you're ready to tell me."

Lloyd stared into the fire; Rye sipped leisurely.

"It was seven years ago, miss, in a back alley in London. I had left a pub after a full evening and was quite inebriated. A block away I was accosted by three men. Mr. Warner entered the fray after one of them had held me, another kicked me in the groin and another slashed my face several times with his pocketknife." He rubbed a finger over several of the scars, then over the bridge of his nose. "Mr. Warner dispatched them one by one, quite handily, I must say."

Paige laid her hand over his, which was clenched on his thigh. "Why did they do that? Did they know you?"

"No, miss. But they knew the pub catered to a certain clientele, one they found immoral."

His fist tightened further. Paige spoke softly to him. "And they were afraid of what they didn't understand," she said, and saw him relax. He was trusting her with his most intimate confidence. She wouldn't violate that confidence. Her thoughts strayed to Rye, who had stood by this gentle man for all these years, and her admiration for him doubled.

"Yes, miss. Mr. Warner took me to hospital and waited through all the tests and X rays. He persuaded me it was time to accept who I was and to get sober. He stayed with me through my detoxification, then he brought me here, gave me work and made me build up my body and learn self-defense. I would do anything for him."

"Don't get sentimental, old friend," Rye said, finally entering the conversation. "I did what any decent person would have done."

"As you say, sir." He pushed himself off the couch and nodded to them. "I will see you in the morning."

Paige stood and hugged him. "Thank you for telling me."

He patted her back awkwardly. "You're very kind."

She kissed his cheek and stepped back. "Keep an eye out for Santa."

"Will do, miss. Pleasant dreams."

"He's paid me back a hundred times for my small part in his new beginning," Rye said as they uncovered the food after he'd gone. "I wish he'd stop fussing over me."

"It seems to me that he leads a full, busy life, doing what he likes to do—taking care of others. Don't diminish his need to help. It's what keeps him going, I think. Dealing with prejudice in whatever form takes so much out of a person. Oh, doesn't this all look wonderful!" Lloyd had provided a perfect Christmas eve dinner of prime rib, baked potatoes, steamed carrots, green salad and apple pie.

Rye turned on the radio, found only Christmas carols and snapped it off again.

"Don't you like Christmas music?" she asked.

"I thought it might bother you."

"I love it. I love Christmas in general. I buy the biggest tree I can fit into my house and invite friends over to decorate it. We spend all day at it, then I play carols on the piano and everyone sings. The traditions are important to me."

He switched on the radio again and music filled the room. They ate in silence, concentrating on the delicious meal, avoiding talking about anything important. Paige saw the puzzlement in his eyes, knew he'd like an explanation for her reaction to the holiday and wondered if she could make him understand. She'd never shared the truth with anyone before. Not all of it, anyway. Her father knew a little of what she felt. And understood only some of it.

Would Rye?

But she let the opportunity slip by as they indulged in an after-dinner brandy and a game of backgammon. One more brandy, and one more game. When she splashed another half-inch into her snifter, he questioned her with raised brows.

"I'm not getting drunk," she said.

"I didn't say anything."

"Your es-spress . . . ex-press-shun—" she nodded in satisfaction that she'd gotten the word out "—spoke louder than words."

Rye tried to keep his face free of telltale expression as he studied her before returning to his task of setting up the backgammon board for another game.

"I'm just relaxed," she said, each word succinct. "Are you going to take advantage of me?"

"Nope."

"Darn."

Rye chuckled. He wondered how often she let her hair down like this. Had she ever?

She plopped onto the sofa, then tipped her head back against the cushion. "Do you think I have a nice neck?"

He sent his gaze on a heated journey to follow her profile from nose to abdomen. "Very nice."

"I've been told my legs are good."

Tossing the dice lightly in his hand, he sat back to observe her. "Spectacular."

She lifted her head to stare at him. "And more than one man has said I have a great . . . tush."

"More than one, huh?"

"At least . . ." She lifted one hand and counted out loud, holding up individual fingers as she did. "Four."

"That many?"

"Yup."

"Four would seem to be a consensus, all right."

"That doesn't count construction workers or stevedores, of course."

"Of course."

"They're extra. But they don't really count."

"No?"

"They whistle at all the women."

"Not all."

"Most," she conceded.

He smiled.

"You're the first man to like my breasts," she said seriously.

"That can't possibly be true."

"Were you being kind to me?"

"No, Paige. I wasn't being kind."

"Prove it."

"I proved it last night."

"I've waited all my life for you," she said with utmost conviction. "All my life."

He gauged her expression as sincere, although the hiccup that had punctuated her sentence destroyed any serious consideration he might have given her announcement. "Why have you, Harry?"

"Because... Because... What was the question?"

Laughing, he folded up the game case, latched it and set it aside. He moved to add a bit of her courage into his own snifter, turned off the radio and all the lights, then sat beside her again. Only the fire provided illumination, shadowing her face, highlighting cheekbones and long, silky lashes. He was about to take shameless advantage of her relaxed state.

"The question was, why have you waited all your life?"

"Waited for what?"

He shook his head. "Why are you still a virgin?"

"Oh, thaaat." She nodded, then went silent.

"Well?"

"Well, what?"

"Paige." He stopped himself before he got angry. She wasn't herself. There was the brandy, of course. But he believed she was using it to hide behind whatever demons haunted her at Christmastime. He watched as she tipped the glass up and drained the last smooth drop. He took the snifter from her and set it with his on the table.

"Is it hot in here?" she asked, plucking at her T-shirt before fanning her face. "I'm really hot."

Before he could stop her, she peeled off the shirt and tossed it dramatically aside, revealing that damned cotton undershirt. At least her nipples weren't protruding. She shifted to sit cross-legged and leaned her elbows on her knees, creating a huge gap he could see into, including the perfect twin roundness beneath.

His gaze traveled up her. "Tell me about your mother and Christmas," he said.

She frowned. "My mother was an angel."

"Undoubtedly. Why is Christmas so important to you?"

She closed her eyes, as if recalling a long-stored image. Suddenly she broke into an a cappella version of "Silent Night," her voice true and clear, piercing in its loveliness. When she finished she smiled beatifically at him.

"That was beautiful," he said.

"That was the last song I sang for my mother."

So, she wasn't as drunk as she seemed, he thought.

"I was the reason she and Daddy got married, you know."

"Your father loved your mother."

"Oh, of course. Beyond life. But she was pregnant. That's why they got married."

"So young," he added.

"And that's the reason I'm still— Am I still a virgin after what we did last night?"

"Technically," he said, his mouth quirking one-sidedly.

"It was wonderful." She closed her eyes and smiled. "Did I tell you how wonderful it felt?"

"You didn't need to."

"Did it feel as good to you?"

Damn. He was getting hard thinking about it. He wanted answers to his questions, not for her to innocently arouse him with reminders of what they'd shared. "It felt every bit as good. Let's talk about something else."

"I think we should do it again."

"I don't."

"It could be my Christmas eve present." She smiled angelically.

"Then tomorrow you'd ask for a Christmas day present."

"You're that good, huh?"

He laughed, exasperated. "Harry, I think you should go to bed and sleep this off."

"Do you? I thought you wanted to know why I've saved myself all these years."

Not drunk at all, he decided. She was as focused as ever. Why the game? he wondered.

"My parents used two—count 'em, two—kinds of birth control. I was conceived anyway."

"Is that the truth, or is that what Patrick has told you all these years?"

Paige opened and shut her mouth. She frowned. "Do you think it was his way of keeping me pure?"

"Seems a possibility, knowing your father."

"You may be right," she said in wonder. "Well, it sure worked. For a long, long time I avoided the temptation because I knew the same thing would happen to me. If my mother was that fertile, so was I. It's in the genes, right?"

"Maybe. What about later? Through college and the years since?"

"I'm not sure I can explain it well. It got to be habit, for one thing. After that, it became a point of pride."

"Pride? In what way?"

"That I could avoid the temptation."

"In the same sense as you test yourself with chocolate, you test yourself with sex?"

She sat back. "I never thought about it that way, but I suppose so."

"Yet you wanted to sleep with *me.*"

"I still do."

"Why?"

"I think I've figured out over the last few days that life is too short to stay a virgin." That sounded like a good answer, a convincing answer, she decided. Would he buy it?

She couldn't tell him she loved him. He'd back farther away than he already had.

"And I'm here and convenient?" he pressed.

"Well—" she dragged the word out "—proximity helps."

"So, if Joey Falcon popped back into your life right now, you'd sleep with him?"

Uh-oh, he was on to her. He knew she didn't want anything to do with Joey, ever.

"Because if you're that anxious to rid yourself of this burden, I figure I've at least got squatter's rights."

She crossed her arms over her chest. "Barbarian."

"Tease," he countered. "You're playing in the big leagues here, Harry. Rookie against veteran, who do you think is gonna win?"

Ten

Paige considered his challenge. She moved to kneel on his thighs, her bottom resting on her heels. Her palms glided down his arms to capture his hands, and she drew them unresisting to cover her breasts, flattening her hands over his. Sucking in a long breath, she closed her eyes as he took over, his hands massaging her flesh, his thumbs brushing the taut peaks. He braced her ribs and helped her raise up; she arched her back as he pushed up her shirt, then his tongue circled the pebbled flesh. She moaned as he drew it into his mouth, clasped his head in her arms as he made a damp trail to the other breast.

"Shall I show you another way it can happen?" he asked gruffly, his meaning coming clear as he slid a hand down her body to cup her damp heat.

Everything they had talked about, everything she'd thought about over the evening had amounted to hours of foreplay. She was as ready as he would ever need her to be, and she groaned as she tipped her pelvis toward him.

"Take responsibility for your actions," he said hoarsely. "Don't just move your body. Give me the words, too. I don't want you throwing this back at me tomorrow."

"Show me something new," she whispered.

After another minute of suckling her, he abandoned her breasts to peel off her leggings as he shifted her to lie flat on the couch. She was wearing the midnight-blue bikinis that he had unwillingly admired as they had dried over the shower rod. Frustrated by the narrowness of the couch, he yanked the pillows off and tossed them aside.

He knelt between her legs, drawing the long limbs around his hips, leaving her undershirt pushed up high, her breasts free to gaze upon. He trailed his fingers along the edges of her panties, dipping under the elastic to touch lightly, retreating to where cloth and skin met, holding her still as she jerked at the contact. Again and again he teased her, her scent assailing him, until she was writhing, lifting herself to meet his fingers. Finally, he dipped farther, discovering her slick heat and gliding upward. Down. Up. Slowly, painstakingly, loving the sounds she made and the way her hips rose and sought a deeper contact, he cherished the pure femininity of her, letting her discover what it was to be a woman wanted by a man.

Whatever insecurities she may have had at the beginning disappeared as he whispered encouragement to her to let go and enjoy it. Her head rolled side to side; her nipples knotted. He used his thumbs to seek and press her sensitive flesh, drawing gasps of pleasure from her, almost killing himself in the process, a test of his inner strength. Finally, he let his thumbs glide up to bracket her responsive bud and she arched up. He reveled as she climaxed hard against the pressure of his hands, her wordless sounds echoing in the silent room.

She lay before him, her arm thrown across her eyes, her chest heaving. He tugged her undershirt down and slid out from under her, scooping up his snifter and taking it to the table to pour a healthy draft into it. The scent of her was on his hand as he brought the glass to his lips. The liquor burned as it went down, too much, too fast.

He took long, tight strides into the bathroom to start the water running in the tub. He picked up the bottle of bubble bath from the counter, poured some in and watched the froth grow for a few seconds, then he returned to the living room and found her sitting cross-legged on the couch.

"Your bath will be ready in a minute," he said, his voice sounding foreign to himself.

"What about you?"

"I'll shower later."

"I meant . . ." Her gaze dropped to about waist level. "About that. You. You know."

He smiled without humor. "I'll live."

"But I've heard that it hurts."

"Hurts?"

"To be aroused and not . . . fulfilled."

"Well, Ms. Full of Experience, don't believe everything you hear. It's not painful, just . . . difficult to reverse."

He watched her climb off the couch and walk to him. Her hands framed his face. Her eyes were filled with something he didn't want to acknowledge, much less believe. It was desire, that was all. Nothing more than plain old lust.

"I want it to be you," she said softly.

"You've waited this long. You can wait for the man you marry."

She flinched at the rejection, but she slid her hands down to rest against his chest. "What's a little loss of innocence between friends?"

He shoved her hands away. "It's everything. Don't you see that? God, Paige. I won't let you use the situation we're in to make life-altering decisions that you'll come to regret tomorrow."

"I won't regret it."

"You don't know that."

"I know it."

He turned from her. "Your bath should be ready."

There was silence behind him for several seconds, followed by the touch of her hand gliding down his back. "Thank you for the Christmas eve present," she said, before walking around and past him, giving him a full view of absolutely perfect legs and the finest rear he'd ever seen. As the bathroom door shut behind her, he swung a fist through the air and swore, a grating rush of sound that hung heavily over him until he finally found retreat in sleep.

"The rain's stopped."

Rye's words accompanied his toss of several boxes onto Paige's bed at six o'clock Christmas morning. She jolted up, then pressed her hands to her head, fighting a morning-after headache, he presumed. And was glad about. At least she was suffering, too, if for a different reason than he.

"Merry—"

"Shhh." She turned a hand palm out. Her eyes were closed.

"Christmas," he whispered, grinning. "What's the matter? Brandy coming back to haunt you?" He wandered into the bathroom, got some aspirin and a glass of water to bring to her.

She swallowed the pills. "Thanks," she said quietly, returning the glass as she leaned against the pillows. "Merry Christmas to you, too."

"I brought you presents."

Her eyes blinked open, and he watched her focus on the pile of wrapped gifts nestled in the comforter.

"But I don't have anything for you," she said, dismayed.

"You don't? Well, I guess I'll have to take mine back." He reached for the smallest box and she batted his hand away.

"There's no sense letting good presents go to waste," she said, a mischievous smile curving slowly upward.

"How do you know they're good?"

"Because anything Lloyd picked out will be good." Her expression said, "Gotcha."

"But he only followed instructions. *Detailed* instructions. The same instructions, by the way, that you could have given him if you'd wanted to surprise me for Christmas, as well."

Her face fell. "I'm sorry. Really. I didn't think—"

"I'm kidding, Harry. We couldn't predict how long we'd be here. Go on, open them."

The first gift made her look in puzzlement at him. The second made her smile. The third made her laugh. The fourth made her throw her arms around his neck and kiss his cheek.

"So, have you guessed what we're doing today?" he asked, untangling her arms from him and setting her back, away from temptation. The pink flannel pajamas had become like a red flag to an inflamed bull. He wanted to charge.

"How long do I have to get ready?"

He pushed himself off the bed. "Take your time. Lloyd will be here soon with breakfast. I've already showered."

He heard her hum and sing, even occasionally chuckle as she showered and did whatever mysterious things she did to look and smell so good.

She opened the bedroom door a crack. "Do you have a pair of pliers?"

"Yeah. Hang on a sec." He pulled them out of a case and passed them through the crack.

"Lloyd's eye was a little off this time," she said as she shut the door.

In a few minutes she emerged, looking cocky, swaggering a bit. "Hey, dude."

Rye settled his fists low on his hips and looked her over. Her hair was pulled into a ponytail on top of her head, a geyser of springy curls. From one ear dangled an earring shaped like a dagger, from the other, a skull. Her lips were

coated with pinkish black lipstick, and her body encased in
black leather and silver chains. As was his own.

Paige laughed when she saw him, dressed so similarly to
her. He hadn't shaved, and combined with the menacing
outfit and the hair he'd gelled into spikes, he looked like he
ate ninety-eight pound weaklings for breakfast.

"Yo, mama," he said, moving in a circle around her to
look at her from every angle. "You wanna put some pants
on over that skin?"

She grinned. "I needed the pliers to pull the zipper up.
Pretty tight, huh?"

He bobbed his head several times and gave her a thumb's-
up. "Perfectamundo."

His boots sported big heels and thick soles, adding a
couple inches to his already imposing height. She felt dainty
in comparison. "So, where are we going?"

"We're gonna get on my Harley and fly. All day, all night,
if you want. Wherever. Whatever. The day is yours."

Tears stung her eyes. He was giving her a different kind
of Christmas, one to replace what she was missing, one so
opposite she wouldn't even think about home. She didn't
think she'd ever met a kinder man than he. "Thank you,"
she whispered past the lump forming in her throat. "I wish
there was something I could do for you."

"Seeing you like this is gift enough," he said. He grabbed
a handful of curls, squeezed, then let go, watching as the
curls sprang back to life. "How'd you do that to your
hair?"

"Actually, it's a matter of what I didn't do. All this curl
is natural. I just control it every day."

"Why?"

"Because it's so unbusinesslike and frivolous."

But you look so much more approachable and fun, he
thought. "Is that what takes you so long every morning to
get ready? Straightening your hair?"

"Hair. Makeup. The works."

"Trust me on this one, Harry. The natural look suits you. Now, breakfast. Lloyd said to wish you a happy Christmas and he was sorry he couldn't stay to see the motorcycle mama. He's helping fix Christmas dinner at the shelter."

They rushed through the meal. Before they left the cottage, they donned big black motorcycle helmets.

"You're walking too ladylike," he observed as they went through the front door. "You're supposed to be one tough dudette, okay? Scuff your feet as you move. Do that swagger thing you did when you came out of the bedroom this morning."

"I can't help but do that a little. The pants are so tight I can't walk right anyway. Oh, my!"

A monster of a bike awaited them, gleaming chrome and black, looking powerful and dangerous. Anticipation vibrated down her spine.

"Harry, meet Harry," he said, his words muffled by his helmet, his gaze unreadable through the black acrylic mask.

She tried to see in. "You named your bike Harry?"

"Yeah. I christened her the day I got her. A year ago."

"Why?"

"Because she's full of sass."

"I don't believe you."

He put a hand against his chest. "I really did name her Harry."

"Oh, I believe that. Just not your reason. Tell me the real one."

His body language broadcasted his discomfort. She thought for a minute he wasn't going to answer, then he muttered, "Because she starts up with a roar, then when I tease her a little, she purrs."

"*What?*"

"You asked."

"But we hadn't met in person. How—"

"It's what I imagined."

"Are you telling me the truth?" She stared at him as he stood Darth Vader-like before her. He had fantasized about her? Just as she had—

"The truth. The whole truth. And nothing but the truth." He angled toward her. "Did you ever fantasize about me?"

"Can I take the Fifth on that?"

He tugged on his leather gloves. "So you've answered my question, and I've answered yours. Let's go see the city."

It was a day she knew she would never forget. She concentrated on the powerful vibration of the bike under her and her chest and stomach pressed against his back. She loosened her death grip on him after an hour or so of riding and learned to relax into the turns. Some of the steeper hills made her stomach do flip-flops, but she fought the fear to laugh joyfully as they zoomed around San Francisco. They ate lunch while watching sea lions frolic over and around Seal Rock, avoided tourist areas and saw people laden with gifts being greeted by others who came running out of houses to hug them, calling out Christmas greetings.

Paige was having the most wonderful Christmas of her life. She loved watching Rye scare the daylights out of a couple of curious kids who stared at them a little too long. He had glowered at the boys, looking fierce and intimidating, his scruffy beard perpetuating the image. She loved sitting with him in silence watching the ocean pound against the rocks and the sea gulls gliding overhead. She loved the sturdiness of his back when she laid her head against him. She loved him. Period.

Which was why when he asked a question about her mother, she finally opened up to him as they sat in Golden Gate Park, half hidden among some bushes, sheltered from the wind.

"I think because you've lost a parent you might understand how I feel better than anyone can. I know you were much older, so you had a chance to really know your father. I didn't have that chance. I had just turned four when my mother died. She'd been sick for a while, and in the hospital most of the time. But she insisted on coming home for Christmas, so my grandfather, my father and I spent a week decorating every room. Dad brought her home on Christmas eve. It was snowing, and we had a fire going, and eggnog, and cookies that some neighbor ladies baked."

She watched a family wobble by on new in-line skates, laughing and teasing each other. "She was so fragile, like an angel. Dad called her his spirit of Christmas, and that's the way I've always remembered her—as a spirit so light and ethereal that a gentle breeze could have lifted her to heaven. I wanted more than anything for her to hold me. I'd missed her so very much. But it hurt her to be touched, so I had to sit on a chair beside her bed. When she slept, I'd pet her hair."

"That's a lot for a little girl to go through," Rye said quietly, curling a hand over hers.

"I couldn't understand why she wasn't the mommy she'd always been. What I remember now of her is mixed up in real memories, dreams and what my father has told me. I can hardly separate truth from fantasy anymore. And I hate that I can't remember what she was really like. I just have vague images of an angelic smile and tissue-paper skin over bone.

"I sang to her, that much I know for sure. And she'd close her eyes and listen, then say how pretty my voice was. Those are the only words I remember, how pretty my voice was. We didn't have presents that year, and I tried not to resent it. But all my friends had something new to wear, and I had a mother I didn't know anymore. It seemed so unfair. When I said so to my father he got furious. I remember him towering over me, so angry. I know now he was hurting even more than I was, but he also didn't understand that I didn't know this woman he'd brought home. She wasn't my mother. She was a shadow of a woman I'd known."

"You were four years old. What's fair and unfair are defined in black and white at that age," he said.

His argument pierced her. Maybe she'd always wanted someone to say it was okay, that her ambivalent feelings for her mother were natural. Long-held resentment began to surface and she fought its arrival. "I have tried to honor my mother with Christmas every year, to celebrate it to the limit. But I think—" She stopped as she began to tremble.

"Go on, Paige. Say it."

"I think I really hate her." She pushed her hand against her mouth, horrified. "Oh, God, that sounds so awful. I didn't hate her. I loved her."

"But you hated what her dying did to your life."

"Yes," she whispered. She swallowed. "And ever since then, I've tried to be what I thought she'd want me to be, what my father expected of me. But I'm not her."

"Does your father expect it—or do you?"

"I don't know." How do you live up to a paragon's example? she wanted to ask. How could she come out from behind her mother's shadow and be her own woman? Would Rye, of all men, be the one to let her? "I just know that I've come to resent the words 'your mother' when they precede some story my father tells, or some comparison he makes."

Rye looked at her bowed head, at the eruption of ringlets that the breeze lifted and tossed. She hadn't ever really played before, he could see that clearly now. She hadn't let herself or hadn't known how, which came from having grown up too fast. Their jaunts to the pistol range, the gym and now today were wholly new experiences. Had she ever in her life done something spontaneous? Had the memories of her mother caused her to suppress the girl in her so much that she had no idea that girl even existed?

You can't do anything about that, he cautioned himself. *It's her life and her choice. You are not responsible for her beyond this assignment.* He repeated the words like a mantra as he fought the vulnerability she'd gifted him with. He didn't need this. On top of physical attraction and the fact he just plain liked her, he didn't need to feel sympathy for her or to make her life different. Better.

So he sat quietly beside her, letting her work it out herself, offering only the support of his hand wrapped tightly around hers, not giving her a shoulder to cry on.

Paige fought disappointment that he hadn't taken her in his arms and comforted her. She'd confided everything to him, and he'd listened calmly, debated logically, then kept his distance. She regretted that she'd told him anything.

"I'd like to go back now," she said. "I haven't talked to my father today, and I need to. I'd almost forgotten why I'm here, and the fact that my life is in danger."

Surprise flickered in his eyes, but he stood, pulling her up with him. He glanced at his watch and was about to say something when his pager vibrated. After checking the digital number he said they had to find a telephone.

"I wouldn't have taken you out today if I thought there was any threat to you," he told her as they climbed on the motorcycle.

"I didn't accuse you of anything."

"You implied that I'd forgotten. I haven't. Dressed as we are, I don't think even your father would recognize us."

"I'm tired."

He started the bike and revved the engine. She resisted the temptation to snuggle up to him as they zipped along until he spotted a phone booth. She watched as a smile stretched across his face, fanning wrinkles at the corners of his eyes. He slammed down the phone and grinned at Paige.

"I'm an uncle!"

"Are you sure we should be in here looking like this?" she whispered to him as they walked the halls of the hospital where his sister had given birth. They'd already had the Pink Lady at the reception desk cowering in her chair, then everyone on the elevator had pushed and shoved their way to the back of the car.

"I can't leave you alone. I can't have you recognized. What's the alternative? And yes, I'm being selfish, but I want to see the baby."

A white-haired lady inching a walker down the corridor looked up from concentrating on her task. Her face drained of color. Paige smiled apologetically at her, and the woman took off, undoubtedly breaking her own land-speed records. Nurses gave them a wide berth.

Paige began to understand the word "pariah." Outcasts, outlaws, out-and-out criminals, that's what they looked like as they tromped down the quiet hallways of the hospital, all creaking leather, jangling chains and thudding boots.

"Here it is, 409."

She followed him into the room because she had no choice.

"Bryan?"

The woman's voice held uncertainty then spilled into a laugh as he descended on her and swallowed her up in an enormous hug.

"Congratulations, sis. How're you feeling?"

"I'm great. I'm wonderful." She looked over Rye's shoulder at Paige, who waved halfheartedly. "What's with the costume?"

He backed away, noticed the man who stood contemplating him from across the bed and moved to engulf him in a hug, as well. "Iain. How'd you do? Did you faint?"

The man with the chestnut hair and brilliant turquoise eyes laughed at Paige, knowing Rye's question was rhetorical. "Who've you got with you?"

Rye turned on his heel and fired a grin her way. "This is Harry. Harry, meet my sister Kani and her husband, Iain MacKenzie."

"Harry?" Kani repeated weakly, eyeing the leather and chains and vicious-looking earrings. She had the same coloring as Rye—mink-colored hair shot with gold and gold-dusted brown eyes that looked tired but elated.

"Hi." The less said, the better, Paige decided.

"So?" Rye crossed his arms over his chest.

"So, what?" Kani asked, grinning.

"Do I have a niece or a nephew?"

Iain picked up a piece of folded fabric and tossed it at Rye. "Put that on and we'll introduce you."

Rye shrugged out of the leather jacket.

"Bryan! You've got a gun? In a hospital? Is that legal?" Kani asked, her voice growing softer with every word.

Iain glanced at the weapon then at Rye as he slipped into the hospital gown. "I'm sure he has his reasons," he said, turning to lift the blanketed bundle from a nearby bassinet. Gently, he put the baby in Rye's arms.

"Meet Kali, your niece."

Paige's heart stopped at the look on Rye's face as he repeated her name and moved the blanket away from her tiny face with his fingers. "Kali. She's beautiful."

"Her name means energy, in Sanskrit," Iain said. "Which is really appropriate, because she came out doing aerobics."

Rye smiled at his sister and brother-in-law before turning his back on them and walking to the window, where only Paige could see his face—and the tears that had gathered in his eyes. He rocked his niece softly, uttered nonsense sounds and unobtrusively brushed at his damp cheeks.

If she hadn't already loved him, she would have fallen in love with him right in that moment.

"Harry?" Kani said hesitantly, her brow furrowed with curiosity. "Would you like to hold her?"

Startled, Paige could say nothing, just glanced from the woman who looked so much like Rye to the man himself, who had turned with a question in his own eyes.

She cleared her throat. "Yes, I'd like to very much, if you're sure?"

"I'm sure. Iain will give you a gown."

She couldn't take off her jacket as Rye had because she wore only her cotton camisole underneath, there being no room for anything else under the tight-fitting garment.

When the chains got caught on the sleeves, Iain had to help her work it over her jacket. Finally covered, she extended her arms to Rye.

Cautiously, a little fearfully, she accepted the sleeping bundle—and fell in love again. She was so tiny, so precious, with her thatch of brown hair that stood straight up and her pink rosebud mouth. Her hands were curled into fists, one at each side of her neck.

"Oh, she's so beautiful," Paige said to the proud parents, who held hands and watched. "She looks just like Kani."

"Do you think so? I thought she looked like Iain right after she was born."

"Right. Squalling and kicking, she looks like me. Peaceful and sleeping, she looks like Kani."

"Can I do anything for you?" Rye asked, taking his eyes off Paige and how right she looked holding a baby. Her fascination with the infant was too tempting.

"Actually, you could," Iain said. "We've been here for over twenty-four hours. Gypsy's probably starving. Would you mind stopping by and feeding her? Leave enough dry food to last until late tonight."

"Oh! She opened her eyes," Paige said in wonder, then moved to Rye's side so that he could see. As the infant's blue eyes moved side to side, her mouth began to make sucking sounds. "I think she wants to eat."

Kani extended her arms to receive her daughter. "I think she'd cry if she was hungry. I'll wait a little while. It's fun just to hold her."

Paige reluctantly gave up the little girl and stepped back. Her gaze connected with Kani's. "I don't usually dress like this," she said.

"Let me guess. You were out of the country during Halloween, and you're making up for missing it." She grinned at her brother.

"We're on the lam," he answered dramatically. "Got some bad guys after us."

"Yeah, right," she said with a quick laugh.

Paige noticed that Iain looked consideringly at Rye, rather than with humor, before he shifted his gaze to Paige, his expression as if to say, "He's telling the truth, isn't he?"

She shrugged.

"So, when's Mom descending?" Rye asked Kani.

"Ten o'clock tomorrow morning. Would you like to pick her up at the airport?"

"I'm really sorry, sis. I can't. I may not even get to see you for a few more days."

"Why?"

"I'm on a job. As soon as it's over, I'll be around."

They left a few minutes later and drove to Kani and Iain's house, a beautiful old three-story Victorian painted dusty rose, its gingerbread trim decorated in ivory, moss green and deep blue. A wreath of dried flowers reflecting the home's colors hung invitingly on the door.

When they were inside, Rye called Gypsy's name, but the cat was playing hide-and-seek with them. Rye disappeared through doorways, hunting, leaving Paige to wander around. That Kani's interest ran toward the work of street artists and unique crafts was obvious in the variety of items that shouldn't have gone together but strangely did, and she had no doubt that Kani, and not Iain, had done the decorating. He would have chosen Shaker furnishings, she decided. Uncluttered lines, bare essentials, fine craftsmanship. Kani reached out to the world.

When Rye climbed the stairs two at a time, she followed more slowly to glance in each open door to the room within. A guest room, a bathroom, then the nursery, which was an inviting vista of the heavens. A grinning sun was painted on one side of the room, the background pale blue and dotted with clouds; a quarter-moon smiled from the opposite wall in a field of purplish-blue dotted with silver stars. The ceiling connected the two shades in a fading spectrum of blues, deep midnight to high noon.

Over the crib dangled a mobile of stars, quarter-moons and suns, and Paige spun the tinkling object. Obviously, the galaxy had some particular meaning for Kani and Iain. She picked up a soft sculpture court jester from atop the batik crib quilt and hugged it as she stared at the rest of the room. Pulling open a tiny drawer, she found sweaters and hats. In the next drawer, stretchy sleepers and drawstring sacques, and the tiniest T-shirts she'd ever seen.

The room already smelled sweetly of baby powder. Paige wondered whether her own mother had anticipated her birth as much as Kani. Had she had a nursery? Had it smelled of baby and love like this room? Had she been frightened? She'd been only seventeen at the birth; she must have been petrified. Paige was a little leery of the process, and she was twenty-eight.

She propped the jester gently on the quilt and walked downstairs. She caught up with Rye as he emptied a can of cat food into a dish, a gray cat weaving around and between his legs.

"Where'd you find her?" Paige asked.

"Behind the dryer, hiding. She knows me because Kani had her when we still shared my house, but I think the boots and chains scared her."

"You and Kani were roommates?"

"Yep. For ten years."

"How fun."

"Yeah, it was." He smiled fondly. "She's a collector of strays, though. Almost every time I came home from a trip, someone new was living there. Teenage runaways, most of the time." He filled two small bowls with dry food for the cat and refilled a larger water bowl. "Okay, let's go. I don't want to hang around any longer than necessary."

"I want to call my father. Can we do it from here, where I can have some privacy, please?"

He stared at her for several seconds, then he crooked a finger and she followed him into a room that was obviously Iain's office. She waited a little impatiently as he completed

:he double series of numbers, then he passed the phone to
ner.

"I'll go far enough away that I can't hear your conversation," he said. "But, please, keep it brief."

She nodded and heard the phone being picked up on the
other end.

Eleven

———

"Hi, Dad," she said when he answered. "Merry Chr—"

"Where the hell have you been?" he roared. "I've left nine messages for Rye. Nine!"

"I'm sorry. We've been out."

"Out? *Out?* Hell, kid. You had me worried out of my mind!"

"I'm sorry," she repeated. "We're fine. We were well disguised."

"Okay, okay. I'm sorry I yelled." She could hear the squeak of his desk chair as he settled back down, so she knew he was in his office at home. She could see him frantically making calls and running his hands through his hair.

"You're doing all right?" he asked, calmer.

She hesitated. "I guess so."

"Something on your mind, Paige?"

"I don't want to keep you, Dad. I know you'll go to the Winchesters' for dinner."

"Spit it out, kid."

She tiptoed around what she wanted to ask. "Were you, I mean, was Mother scared to have me?"

"Scared in what way?"

"Through the pregnancy and delivery."

The chair squeaked loudly. "What are you asking? You're not—"

"Of course not, Dad. I've just been thinking about Mother, and me as a baby, and if it was awful being parents so young."

"You were wanted and loved, honey, from the very beginning."

"But you had to get married. It must have been difficult."

It was his turn to hesitate. "I know I've told you all your life that we had to get married. To be honest, I thought it would prevent you from making foolish mistakes as a teenager."

"It worked," she admitted. "What's the truth?"

"The truth is that your mother's family was moving to Dallas. She didn't want to move; they wouldn't let her stay. We intentionally got pregnant so they had no choice but to leave without her."

Paige didn't know how to react. "I was a means to an end?"

"We were kids. We loved each other. We knew we'd get married eventually but we had no power because of our ages. It was our way of living our own lives. We never regretted it or you."

"Did I have a nursery?"

"A nursery? Let me think. We lived with your grandfather, you know. Well, I guess you could call it that. You had your own bedroom."

"But was it decorated for a baby? Did it smell like baby powder?"

"I don't remember. What's going on, Paige? Why do you sound next to tears?"

"I'm just missing my mother all of a sudden. The history. My history."

"Is it Rye? Is he putting some pressure on you?"

She hesitated. "All these years I've had a picture of him in my mind," she said quietly, "and it's always been larger than life. The funny thing is, he matches my image. He is larger *in* life. But he's also very kind, very down to earth. Normal."

The chair squeaked a hundred decibels louder as he obviously sprang out of it. "Don't you believe it, honey. That man is trouble. You got that? Trouble. He's not for you."

Paige bristled. "Why not?"

"He just isn't, that's all. He'll break your heart, kid. Believe me, he will. You just don't . . . fit."

"Why not? I'm not sophisticated enough for him? Or cosmopolitan enough? Or sexy enough?"

"Don't talk to me about sexy. I don't want to hear this. He'd better not be taking advantage of you in your situation, when you can't make logical decisions—"

"Now, wait a minute, Dad. First of all, he hasn't taken advantage. Secondly, who says I haven't kept my head about me? I'm not some brainless—"

"What about Joey Falcon?"

"What about him?" She knew what he meant, but she was stalling for time and the right argument. "He was . . . temporary insanity. I'm back to normal now."

"It sure as hell doesn't sound like it to me."

"It's my business, though, isn't it?"

"I knew it! Paige, honey, don't do this. It would be the biggest mistake of your life. I'm telling you. I've been out drinking with the man, and believe me—"

She laughed. "Drinking buddies, are you? What's that, some kind of all-night brag session? Well, I don't want to make you late for dinner. Talk to you later. Bye."

She dropped the phone as if it was flammable. Furious, she pushed herself out of the chair and stalked to the window. How dare he! How dare he imply she was some flighty woman without a mind of her own, without a *sensible* mind of her own. Sometimes he was such a—

A knock sounded at the door. "We really should go, Harry. We've been here too long already."

She flung open the door and stormed past him.

"What's wrong?" he asked as he followed.

"My father. He can be such a *jerk* sometimes."

"You're just finding that out?" He caught her by the elbow and slowed her down so that she wouldn't draw attention to herself. "Put your helmet on."

They climbed aboard the Harley, and Rye started the engine. As he turned to look over his shoulder before pulling away from the curb he spotted a man sitting in a plain, dark sedan one house away, watching them intently. Rye focused on the license plate, then took off in the opposite direction. In his mirror, he saw the car make a U-turn and follow. Rye lost him within ten seconds.

Halfway back to the hotel he remembered the other gift he'd arranged for her, a gift that would have been delivered that morning if the rain hadn't complicated matters, and he suddenly hoped Lloyd hadn't been able to locate it after all.

The ride back to the cottage blew the anger out of her, replacing it with weariness. She leaned against his back, feeling tired and alone, thinking that her father was never going to acknowledge her as a fully functional, competent woman, capable of rational thought. And what about Rye? She had bared her soul to him and had needed his sympathy, but he hadn't offered it. He confused her with his moments of understanding and thoughtfulness that were so often followed by a step backward. She wanted her uncomplicated life back. And her freedom.

When she felt the motorcycle turn and slow way down, she lifted her head and caught a glimpse of something in front of the cottage. Something white . . . and heaped beside the door.

She sat taller and strained to see around him as he rolled to a stop and turned off the engine.

Mesmerized, she climbed off the bike, pulled off the helmet and took a few steps forward. "Snow," she whispered. "Snow."

She felt him draw near and curve a hand over her shoulder. "I didn't realize until today how very painful Christmas is for you. I had thought the snow might help in some way. I didn't mean to make it harder—"

"You brought me snow. I can't believe you brought me— It's the nicest thing anyone's ever— Oh, God."

She didn't want to cry in front of him, but she couldn't seem to stop the flow of tears sent by her over-full heart to spill out in gratitude and love. Dropping to her knees into the pile of Christmas white, she scooped up two handfuls to press to her cheeks, the stark coldness shocking the tears to a halt.

"Is it all right?" he asked from close behind her.

The uncertainty in his voice made her mouth flicker into a smile. An insecure Rye was something she hadn't dealt with before. There was only one way to break the mood. She fired a snowball over her shoulder—and hit him squarely in the face.

It took about two seconds for him to retaliate, and the resulting fight must have ranked as the quietest in history as they tried not to draw attention to themselves. He managed to stuff a substantial amount of snow down the back of her jacket. She had to settle for shoving a heap under his, against his stomach.

She suspected he had let her have some success, because he certainly could have overpowered her, but it was the most fun she'd had in years. Decades.

Paige wanted to build a snowman, but Rye apologetically said no, and they brushed snow off each other before finding shelter inside the cottage.

Lloyd had come and gone, leaving lasagna for them in the refrigerator and a list of messages for Rye, mostly from Patrick. She showered and changed out of the wet, binding motorcycle leathers into her jeans and sweater, but left her hair in the waterfall ponytail. While Rye made calls to his mother and sister, then one requesting information on a license plate, Paige heated the lasagna and served it, along with a crisp green salad.

Rye didn't know what to make of her. He'd seen a spectrum of emotion in her today, but her almost total silence since they'd entered the cottage made him edgy. "What's wrong?" he asked as he stacked their empty plates together. "I had hoped today would make you happy—"

"I'm so grateful, I can't even begin to express it. It was a wonderful surprise and I'll never forget it. I've just been realizing how much I've missed in life."

He didn't want to hear this. He was sure he didn't want to hear this. But he asked anyway. "Like what?"

She lifted her hands palms up in a helpless gesture. "Fun. Family. Love. When I looked at Kani and Iain and saw the love they so obviously share, and the way it showered onto the new life they'd created, I realized I want that too. Someday."

He closed his eyes briefly. Someday. That answer was okay.

"But I wish...I had someone special in my life. Someone to share things with, like your sister has."

"You will." He moved into the kitchen and rinsed off their dinner dishes, stacking them in the box Lloyd had left. "Cheesecake?" he asked, in an attempt to change the subject.

"Maybe later." She followed him and leaned against the counter. "Don't you ever wish for that?"

"No. Not now. I figure I'll quit doing this kind of work in five more years, before my reflexes slow any and I start making stupid mistakes. Until then, I need to be free to go at a moment's notice. That's not fair to any woman, especially a wife."

"Why couldn't she go with you some of the time?"

He opened his mouth to scoff at the idea, but closed it again. "I suppose she could, occasionally, to certain parts of the world."

Paige smiled secretly. She'd planted the idea, now she would wait and see what came of it. She glanced at her watch. "Seven-thirty. It's too early to sleep, unless you plan on getting me up in the middle of the night again for some new adventure?"

"Not tonight. I feel the same as you, I'm tired but I don't want to sleep yet. I think I'll shower the gel out of my hair. Maybe we can just watch a little television."

"Fine." She pushed away from the counter.

He cupped her arm. "There's something I need to tell you first. When we left Kani and Iain's, there was a man in a dark sedan who seemed to try to follow us."

"Seemed to try to?" she repeated.

"I don't know if it means anything. When we left, he followed us. I lost him right away, but the car's a rental. It's just too coincidental."

"Why would someone be waiting at your sister's house?"

"Maybe there's more than one person on surveillance," he said. "If they're watching Kani's house, someone's undoubtedly watching mine. I'm going to have Lloyd check it out."

"No."

"What?"

"I said no. If they're watching, they're watching. Don't involve Lloyd in this. I'd never forgive myself if he got hurt because of me."

"He's well trained, Paige. He can handle himself."

"It isn't worth it. Please, promise me you won't ask him to do it."

"It could be the lead to break the case open. If we surprise them first."

"If, if, if. I'm begging you not to involve Lloyd. If you insist on checking it out, leave him here with me and you do it. I promise not to lure him into taking me sight-seeing."

"Maybe I'll do just that."

She crossed her arms over her chest. "Fine."

The phone rang. As Rye conversed with her father, telling him about the unknown watcher and Rye's plan to investigate further, Paige decided she was done with attempting to entice him. He obviously had a great deal of inner strength to resist her offer, and it didn't appear that she could do anything to break that self-control, or even bend it.

As he showered, she changed into her pajamas, took the rubber band out of her hair and let the curls fall around her shoulders, then she turned on the television and climbed into bed. When he joined her a few minutes later wearing only sweatpants, his face was free of stubble and he smelled of soap, shampoo and shaving cream. He sat on the bed and stared at her so long that she finally looked herself over, but found nothing out of the ordinary.

"What?" she asked.

"You look different with your hair curling around your face and over your shoulders."

"Different, good or different, bad?"

"Different, sexy."

Paige caught her breath. He was looking at her as if she was an ice cream cone and he had been roaming the desert for years. She plucked at her pajama top. "Yeah, right. This little number is guaranteed to incite uncontrollable urges, all right."

"It sure as hell incites mine."

She sat back. "What's going on, Warner? I've offered myself on a silver platter and you've refused. Have you changed your mind?"

You talked to your father about me, he thought, recalling the phone call of a while ago. *You said something that made him warn me away from you.* Patrick had ordered him to leave her alone, and that made him want her even more. Primitive, no, *primordial* pleasure warred with the long-held feminist beliefs of which he had always been so proud. She had given herself to no other man, and she wanted to give herself to him.

He could cite ten reasons he had finally decided not to resist any longer. But only one mattered—he wanted her. "Why me, Paige?"

She leaned intently toward him. "Because with you I know it will be right and good. Meaningful. A lifetime memory."

It shouldn't please me so much. He never would have expected it, looked for it or dreamed about it, but here it was. His, if he wanted. All his. Only his. "How do you know that?"

"I just do. It's instinctive. I can't describe it. I just know I want it to be you I remember for the rest of my life."

"It would be painful with me, too. There's no way around that."

"Just the first time. I'm inexperienced, not ignorant."

He felt everything within him shatter—his determination to resist her and his resolve that she return to Boston unchanged. He ignored the twinge of conscience that struck him next, because she was right to trust him to make the experience a memorable one. He knew he could. Just the thought of what she was expecting of him and what he knew he could give her excited him beyond sensibility. Still he kept his voice even because tomorrow he'd have to deal with her vulnerability. "The first time," he repeated. "How many times do you expect?"

"As many as it takes to teach me the way of it. As many times as we want. I've heard it takes a while for a couple to really connect. I don't expect miracles," she said seriously.

He groaned, exasperated. "You've heard your share of information and *mis*information, haven't you?"

"I expect you'll set me straight." She glanced at the fire before returning her gaze to him. "I assume you have birth control with you and that you will use it safely and properly. We won't have any surprises waiting for us down the line."

There were no decisions left to make. He pressed the power switch on the remote control, leaving the room humming with silence. No music, he decided. He didn't want music. Only the song of her sighs and whispers, and more. He already knew how responsive she was, how open. Now he could take her as far as he wanted. And he could go with her.

He threaded his fingers through her curls; his palms rested against her cheeks as he lowered his mouth to hers. "I hope there'll be a lot of surprises tonight," he said, brushing his lips lightly back and forth across hers, catching her breath in his mouth, relishing the shuddering response.

"Is this really happening?" she breathed as he trailed her neck with tiny nibbles.

"I promise you, it's not a dream," he answered, then kissed her again, more fiercely, more desperately. She tasted of desire, hot and sweet. Her arms twined his waist; her fingers dipped into the waistband of his sweatpants and traced his spine all the way down. He moved back a little, allowing himself enough space to unbutton the pajama top and send it whispering to the bed. He shoved it aside, stopped to stare at her without touching, savored the way her nipples tightened just from his gaze.

"Stand up," he ordered hoarsely, holding her hand as she complied. He tugged on the pink pants, lowering them slowly, teasingly, feeling her hand on his head for balance as she stepped out of the garment and he swept it aside. When she would have dropped to the bed again, he stopped her and knelt before her, admiring her pale skin as it reflected the firelight, adoring the shape of her breasts, treasuring the long legs and the delicate triangle at their juncture. He leaned forward, her scent drawing him magnetically, uncontrollably to press his lips there.

"Oh, Rye," she sighed as his tongue stroked her, seeking hidden delights. Her legs went wobbly; he clutched her bottom to keep her still and upright. Her palms rested on his head as she tipped her own back and moaned to the ceiling. He brought his fingers into the game, doing clever things with them until she didn't know who she was anymore. She had become a shooting star that wouldn't fade. Suddenly he pulled away, leaving her so close to the far reaches of the galaxy that she cried out.

"There's time," he said, his voice gruff with need.

She sank onto the bed as he plucked a small packet from his back pocket then pushed his sweatpants off and away. She reached for him.

"Don't touch me," he said.

Startled, she went still.

"I'm ready to explode. If you touch me, I will. And I'm doing my damnedest to make this everything it should be for you." He opened the packet as he talked and removed the condom. She watched in fascination as he rolled it down himself, then he reached for her.

Skin to skin, they clung to each other as busy mouths stoked the heat of a smoldering fire. There was no pressure to hurry; each second, each touch, each taste was a luxury of texture and flavor. In the back of his mind, Rye wondered how long it had been since he'd enjoyed just kissing. He had forgotten how the individual shape of lips changed the way mouths could fit together; how the taste could be darkly hot or sweetly enticing; how a trembling breath inhaled and exhaled while mouths were joined could send shivers of ecstasy into deeply buried and feverish nerve endings; how the quest for further intimacy could bring teeth in contact; how a tongue could demand or acquiesce; how a throat could vibrate unintelligible sounds of bliss. He had forgotten—or he had never felt like this before.

"I need to touch you," she said softly, stroking his face over and over.

He groaned, closing his eyes, as the initial reverence in her hands turned greedy and bold, then when she added the aphrodisiac of her mouth, the power shifted solely to her. He gave in to the unfamiliar loss of control, allowing himself the pleasure of her teasing torment. He had forgotten how fingertips could catch fire against skin, leaving trails of ignited desire in their wake; how breath could dust body hair, making it rise and crackle; how lips could mold hard muscle and soft flesh; how a tongue could slither over and around sensitized curves. He had forgotten—or he had never felt like this before.

When even a dust mote against his skin would have tipped him over the edge, he lifted her hands away, willing her to open her eyes.

"My turn," he said in a sandpapery whisper. Everything was new and fresh—the leanness of her body, the fragility of her bones, the delicate scent of her perfume—her bottled trademark and the essence he drew from her. He aimed for gentleness but discovered she wanted him as greedy as she. Her innocence simmered on the back burner of his mind, intruding with proprietary satisfaction, an unfamiliar sensation bound to change his life irrevocably.

He had forgotten how skin could take on the texture of velvet; how a puckered nipple could taste like the deep rose of its color; how an abdomen could become a desert to explore, barren and beautiful; how an inner thigh could breathe a different perfume than a breast, no less enticing, no less intriguing. He had forgotten the unrivaled pleasure of making love with a partner who wanted him more than anything in life. He had forgotten—or he had never felt like this before.

She writhed beneath him, lifting herself toward discovery. But there were a few more things he wanted to introduce her to first, intimate things, consciousness-losing things. As she was giving him the gift of her innocence, so could he give her the gift of time. At last, he held himself above her and tried to control his own trembling as he nudged her legs apart.

"Go slow," she whispered, almost frantic with need. "I want to feel you for as long as you can make it last."

He squeezed his eyes shut and pressed forward, but he wanted so much to watch her face as he made her his that he forced his eyes open. She was watching him, her brows drawn together, her jaw tight and nostrils flared. From her mouth came erratic breaths and tiny sounds he couldn't decipher as pain or need.

He shook everywhere from holding back. Sweat beaded his forehead. He felt the barrier tear, heard the encouragement in her voice, and pressed harder. *Hurry, hurry,* he urged her silently, trying to divert his mind elsewhere. But he was surrounded by her warmth, and her face shone with exultation. Finally, her head fell back, and a long, low moan filtered out of her open mouth. Free to join her, he gathered her close, burrowed his head next to hers and celebrated the same wonderment clear to his soul.

Paige tightened her arms around him as he shifted his body. "Don't go," she whispered, not knowing what else to say. The words *thank you* popped into her mind and were quickly discarded. He moved only enough to rest on his elbows, taking his weight off her while keeping their skin in contact. He slid down to press his cheek to hers; they rested like that for a minute.

"Are you all right?" he asked quietly, drawing her closer and rolling them to their sides.

"I'm perfect."

"You certainly are." He pulled back to kiss the smile on her lips then brushed her cheek with his knuckles. "I'm trying to resist asking stupid questions," he admitted. "Adolescent questions."

She understood his need to know; indeed, she wanted him to know how it felt. "It was a lovely kind of pain," she said with a catch in her voice. "Worth waiting for. Well worth waiting for."

"And after that?"

"How do you describe heaven?" She sighed, smiling slightly as she felt him relax and settle more comfortably into the mattress. "I can't wait until we *really* connect."

His mouth widened by degrees, and she brushed a finger across his lips. "You made it special," she said. "Memorable."

"If you say thank you—"

"Never even crossed my mind," she said, wide-eyed and innocent.

His hand swept down her back and over her right buttock. "I think it did."

Her laugh was short and soft. "So you have me all figured out, do you?"

"Hell, no. I hope I never do. But you're polite to the bitter end."

I hope I never do. Paige latched on to those words and silently let them pierce her soul. Did he even know what he said? Was she making too much of a throwaway line?

"Sleepy?" he asked as she snuggled closer.

"A little."

His hand brushed through her hair. His words were hesitant. "I'm sort of at a loss here, Paige."

She yawned. "In what way?"

"Should I get a washcloth or something?"

Her eyes flew open. Practicality intruded. Of course he'd need to clean up. She could use a hot soak, herself. Or a cold one. She didn't know which. "I guess I should get up," she said finally.

It was an awkward moment. Paige rolled to one side of the bed, Rye to the other. Their gazes were unwillingly drawn to the sheet and its evidence of what had happened. Paige raised her eyes slowly; she took her fill of him before settling her gaze on his face.

"I didn't want it to be so important," he said gruffly. "But, God, Paige, when I felt that barrier inside you give, I wanted to shout it to the world. I never would have thought it of myself. I have this ridiculous urge to hang the bedsheet from the window like they did centuries ago."

"How barbaric," she said, watching him walk around the bed. He swept her into his arms and held her for a long, long time—until she lost any awkwardness at their nudity, until she felt a part of him, until she wanted him again and told him so.

He worried aloud about her tenderness.

She declared the discomfort worth it.

He assured her he was her slave.

Her response was a ladylike snort of disbelief.

Twelve

They'd been caught! Paige tightened her grip on the muscular arm holding her snugly against a solid chest as they'd slept. They were naked, tousled and obviously wallowing in the aftermath of a whole night of lovemaking when Lloyd's key turned the lock on the front door.

Rye awakened simultaneously. "Shh," he said into her hair. "It's all right. Lloyd knew I was attracted to you before I even admitted it to myself."

Stunned, Paige could only lie there and try to pull in enough air to survive.

They'd left the bedroom door open—meaning there was no way Lloyd could miss seeing them in bed together. She peeked over Rye's arm just in time to catch Lloyd's expression.

She saw his gaze sweep the room before stopping to focus on the tiny box that lay on its side on the nightstand, the floor below scattered with several square packets that had spilled in their haste to grab one a little while ago. She had awakened with her mouth pressed to his chest, and she had burrowed under the blankets to awaken him with intimate caresses. He'd let her unroll the condom down him, a process she had found exciting in its intimacy.

Well, who was going to speak first? she wondered, irritated at the silence.

"Good morning, Lloyd," she said finally.

"Miss. *Sir.*" He dragged the word out with chilling precision. "I will leave your breakfast in the kitchen."

"Thanks," Rye muttered as he stretched, seemingly unconcerned. The furnace that his tantalizing chest had made cooled as he pulled away.

Paige wanted to slug him for his utter disregard of her nakedness as the sheet shifted with him and she had to grab on tight.

"I need to speak with you, if I may, sir," Lloyd said from the living room, having turned his back on them and removed himself to a discreet distance from the door.

Rye smiled encouragingly at her, kissed the top of her head, rolled out of bed and slipped into his sweatpants. Paige waited until he shut the door behind him before she jumped out of bed, found the hotel robe in the closet and retreated to the bathroom.

She looked in the mirror, wondering if she'd look different this morning. Her hair was a billboard advertising the last twelve hours—corkscrews springing into the air, rickrack flattened against her head. She was about to turn on the shower when Rye called her name and asked her to come into the living room.

Her gaze coveted her hairbrush and the bathtub, then she sighed loudly and left the room.

"Lloyd says he spotted someone waiting outside my house this morning, in a dark sedan. Any bets the license will check out as a rental?"

"What are you going to do?" She avoided looking at Lloyd, who she could sense was uncomfortable. Damn. She really did feel like a teenager being caught by a parent, even though he'd had a role in making their union possible. It occurred to her that she'd missed too many late-night bubble baths and early-morning meditations during the last few days. Her composure was as close to shattering as it had ever been in her life. "Are you going to confront the man?" she asked Rye.

"Not without police protection. It'll take some arranging. Are you sure you weren't followed here?" he asked Lloyd.

"I assure you, sir, I was not."

"Lighten up, old friend. This is not the end of the world here," Rye said, teasing the solemn man gently.

"Are you all right, miss?" Lloyd asked her directly.

As both men focused so intently on her, she felt her face heat. "I'm fine. Honestly," she added as he frowned.

She watched him turn the fiercest expression she'd ever seen on Rye, a combination of "I told you so" and "How could you?" If she hadn't been so aware of her appearance, she would have hugged him. Her own father rarely expressed such concern.

He bowed tightly and turned to leave.

"Keep in touch," Rye called after him. The door shut with a controlled click.

They both stared at the closed portal.

"Well, that was a little awkward," Rye said. "Are you sure in some past life he wasn't your father?"

She smiled. "He's very kind."

Rye turned slowly her direction and really looked at her for the first time, at the wild hair and cosmetic-free face, an endearing, slightly comical sight. "Morning's not your best time of day, is it?"

"You're so romantic, Warner. I figure I've earned these tangles."

"Have you?" He moved a little closer, caught her lapels and let his hands glide down them, then sent his forefingers on a journey back up the V of visible skin. "The night was incredible," he said sincerely.

"Does it end here? Are you going to take off and be Mr. Secret Agent Man now and leave me alone?"

The tightness of her voice threw him, as if she was suddenly afraid for him to go. He couldn't have that. He wouldn't. *Don't go all female on me now,* he wanted to say. *Stay strong. Be tough. Be the Paige I've come to know and—*

He let the thought trail off in his mind, cursing the attraction that always seemed to accompany a woman's vulnerability. Weakness meant dependency. Dependency meant commitment. Commitment meant forever. He wasn't ready for forever, and certainly not with anyone who would cling to him and make him give up too much of himself.

Paige watched the play of emotions cross his face. He was confused, she decided. And hesitant. About her? About them? Deciding to keep it light between them, she slipped a hand into his sweatpants as his palms cupped her breasts. She wrapped her fingers around him and felt him respond.

"Definitely no loss of reflexes here," she commented. "I think you have longer than five years before you have to worry about it."

He grinned. "Suddenly, you're an expert?"

"I told you I'm not ignorant. If you think I haven't heard tales about sex all my adult life, you're wrong. Women talk about it as much as men, you know."

"Is that so?" He closed his eyes as she continued to hold and caress him. His thumbs teased the tight peaks of her breasts. "So what did you know ahead of time?"

"Oh, I understood some of the male physiology. And something about needs and urges."

"Yet you never gave into them yourself."

"I'm not a man."

He sucked in a breath as she grew a little bolder. "Women have needs, too. Isn't that what the women's movement has accomplished? Acknowledgment that you all have the same urges as men?"

"I'm not all women," she chided him, using his own argument against him. "I'm stronger than the average."

He looked seriously at her. "Can you stay that way?"

She tipped her head to one side as he wrapped a hand around her wrist, stilling it. "What do you mean?"

"I mean, you're not gonna turn all feminine ooze on me now, are you?"

"Ooze?" She considered the word, not understanding his meaning, nor the intensity in his eyes, as if this was the most important question in the universe, one bigger than "What is life?"

"I thought that was the goal," she said. "For us to ooze—"

His hand tightened. "Yeah. You're right. But aren't you sore?"

"Terminally."

His gaze caressed her face, then he swept her into his arms, carried her to the bathroom and stepped directly into the tub, where she enjoyed the most wonderful shampoo of her life.

"The rental car is gone, sir," Lloyd said when Rye answered the phone later. "Shall I stay here and watch? I could call you as soon as it reappears."

"I don't want to tie you up—"

"I think we should do everything possible to end this crisis so that Miss O'Halloran may return home."

"Away from me, you mean."

"I didn't say that, sir."

"The number of times you call me 'sir' is usually a good barometer of how irritated you are with me."

"Indeed, sir?"

"Indeed." Rye listened to Paige humming in the kitchen as she made sandwiches out of the cold cuts, sliced vegetables and sourdough rolls Lloyd had brought with their breakfast this morning. "Frankly, I'm torn between wanting this to end and wanting to draw it out. I don't want the honeymoon called off."

"One is not granted the privilege of a honeymoon without a legal document, sir. What you are enjoying is merely a seduction."

"Ah, but who seduced whom?" Rye asked, feeling himself color.

"In her innocence she knew not what she was doing."

"You've been perturbed with me before, old friend. We don't always agree on the subject of women. So let's drop it."

"I noticed you didn't dispute her innocence, sir."

Rye hesitated. "No. I don't dispute it."

"You have a moral obligation," Lloyd fired back.

"What century did you grow up in? I protected her, as charged. If the protection *fails,* I have an obligation. If not, then the decisions will be up to us. Not you, not society, not fathers or father figures. Clear?"

"Quite. So, I am free to go, sir?"

His voice almost straightened the corkscrew telephone cord.

"By all means." Rye stared at the phone as he cradled the receiver. Lloyd was so irritated with him, he hadn't even said goodbye.

Leaning back against the couch, he rubbed his eyes wearily. Lloyd was right, of course. All night, his obligations had weighed heavily on his mind. For the first time in his memory, his word hadn't been his bond. He had told her he wouldn't have her making life-altering decisions while she was embroiled in this situation, yet he had allowed just that.

He had rationalized making love to her with as fine a debate as he'd ever had with his own conscience. She wanted him to be the one, therefore he was merely obliging her. She had strong feelings for him, strong enough to light Patrick's fuse of parental protectiveness, therefore Rye responded so that Paige would win over Patrick, a rarity that Rye believed she would appreciate. And his ego had convinced itself that he would make her first experience as memorable as she deserved.

He could completely justify his actions—and the fact that he had no obligation beyond the moment. Now, if he could just get rid of Temptation and Duty, who had reappeared on his shoulders during the night and were still giving him hell in both ears.

"What's wrong?" Paige asked as she set their lunch plates on the table and moved to take a seat.

Damn, she was beautiful. Her hair bounced like a first grader let out for recess; her face, still free of makeup, glowed with whatever emotions she harbored; her lithe body moved sensuously, enticingly around the dining table, drawing his gaze all the way down to her hot pink toenails.

"Have you wondered why we haven't met before this?" he asked as he joined her at the table, not answering her question.

"Often. I've asked my father to let me know when you're in town, but he's always had an excuse for why he hasn't. Yesterday on the phone, he warned me off you."

Rye pretended surprise. "Did he? Why? What did he say?"

She looked him straight in the eye. "He said you'd break my heart."

"I must have a hell of a reputation that I'm not aware of." He took a bite of sandwich, making light of Patrick's warning.

Paige noticed his discomfort. He was holding back, as he had been since right after they'd made love for the first time last night. He'd seemed to pour everything into the one time—his need to make it perfect for her had superseded his own pleasure, delaying it much longer than she assumed was usual, and she was grateful. And her love for him had only grown during the long, revealing night.

But he held himself back, as if he expected her to cling, which she absolutely refused to do. Even though she wanted to.

He was a complex man. Intense, focused, logical; kind, tender, unselfish. But not honest—not with her, and not with himself. Why? All her life she'd dealt with a man who wasn't forthcoming with her, although she had to admit, her father played games with everyone. She refused to get involved with another games player.

So, don't toy with me, she warned Rye silently, wishing she had the nerve to bring it all into the open. Maybe when this was all over, but not now. Not when there was so much more to experience, and savor, and treasure.

Night fell, and with it came privacy. There was no Lloyd to drop in unexpectedly. The phone wouldn't ring unless it was an emergency. They built a blazing fire in the living room hearth and were ensconced among pillows and the bedroom comforter on the couch, with Paige settled between Rye's legs, her back cushioned by his chest, her head resting against his collarbone, her curls pillowing his chin. She was blissfully content within the warm shelter of his arms. They had talked of family, and childhood, and adolescence; of awkwardness, and failure, and success.

She trailed her fingers down his arms to the tips of his thumbs. "You must meet a lot of interesting people."

He hooked an arm across her chest; his hand cupped her shoulder. "Oh, yeah. Embezzlers, fugitives, terrorists."

"For every bad guy there must be five good guys, or..."

"Ahh."

"What does that mean?"

"You're really asking about *women* I've met. That's what you meant by interesting people."

"Is that what I meant?"

His chest jostled her as he chuckled softly. His fingers caught the edge of the comforter and tugged until one breast lay bare to his gaze. She followed the path of his finger as he teased her nipple to a taut peak, then drew a deep, quavery breath as he uncovered the other breast. "You're distracting me," she whispered.

He turned her to face him as he sat up straight, pulling her legs along the outside of his, straddling her in his lap. "You are incredibly perfect," he said, just staring, waiting to see if she'd take the initiative.

She fidgeted in his lap, wanting his hands on her, wanting to feel his mouth surround her pebbled flesh. She looped her arms around his neck, bringing herself closer.

"Something you want, Harry?"

"You know I do."

"So tell me. Give me the words."

After a moment of deliberation she managed them. "I ache for you."

The ache intensified, staggeringly so as she watched him suckle and tease and taste, causing a tingling tautness throughout her body. His lips slid to the indentation between her breasts and he took a deep breath. "I've never been involved with a woman during a case, Harry. I don't know why you think differently. I'd never be that dishonest."

"But... what about me?"

"You shatter all my rules. Rules you can't even begin to comprehend. And don't think I haven't beaten myself up about it."

She pushed her fingers into his hair and tipped his head back. She liked the gruffness in his voice; she liked that she'd made him break his own rules and was suffering for it; she liked the feeling of empowerment.

Paige smiled, a slow expression of pleasure. She cradled his head in her arms as she kissed him fiercely, moved rhythmically against him, caused him to pull back abruptly and suck in air. She didn't give him a chance to recover but lunged at him again and again, sliding along him, stopping to taste and savor. He was hotter than fire; she was parched with need. Thirsty, they drank of each other.

She was learning how to hover just at the edge of fulfillment, savoring the last bit of earth for long moments before either backing away and inching toward the edge again, or stepping off into a freefall of delight. She had discovered the beauty of making love, the spiraling pleasure that defied description, followed by the tender aftermath of quiet talk and gentle caresses. But she gloried in the freedom of passion. Everything she'd held in reserve was released in a fury of desire. He felt so good—solid, comforting, enduring, enticing.

"Is it all right...?" she asked repeatedly.

His answer never varied. "Whatever you want."

She wanted the endless moment of fulfillment—her own and his. She wanted it again and again and again. There was no past, no future, only the here and now. There was only this man—protector, friend, lover—and the beautiful memories he gave her.

They had showered and dressed before Lloyd arrived very early the following morning, announcing he'd driven by Rye's house on his way over and that the rental car had returned to its post.

"I need you to stay with Paige," Rye said to Lloyd. "And I want you to guarantee me you'll both be here when I return."

"We will," Paige said, unwilling to let Lloyd get into trouble over her. She'd cool her heels, worry about Rye and wait for the sound of his key in the lock.

She watched him shrug into the shoulder holster that was so much a part of him. He took out the gun, checked it, then slid it into its cradle.

"Eat first," she said. "You don't know how long it will take you."

"I don't want to take the time." His voice trailed off as she bestowed her most commanding look on him. He headed to the table. "And you can wipe that smirk off your face, old friend."

Lloyd's mouth twitched. "I do not smirk, sir."

"Of course not. You just smile with extreme smugness."

Paige's gaze caressed him as he ate. She probably looked like a lovesick adolescent, she decided, unable to control her need to memorize every inch of his face. If anything happened to him . . . She wouldn't think about it. He'd been in worse situations, she was sure, and he had the upper hand in this one. If someone was lying in wait for him, Rye wouldn't be caught off guard. A patrol unit would be waiting a block away from his house and would follow him there.

He kissed her goodbye, nothing short and sweet, but long and lingering. They hadn't been apart for six days. She didn't want the umbilical cut. Unintentionally, she dug her fingers into his back and refused to let him go.

He tried to pull away, and she clutched his jacket and buried her face against his chest.

"Don't, Paige. Please, don't."

"I know you want me to be strong," she said, her voice small and tight. "I'm sorry. Unlike you, I have weaknesses."

He sighed over her head, disturbing fragrant curls that fell back against his face. He'd seen this coming all morning. From the moment he'd announced he would be leaving to check his house, her fears had been advertised as clearly as a marquee announcing coming attractions. She'd grown dependent on him for safety and comfort—and maybe more. He continued to fight it all. "I have my own weaknesses," he admitted. "Everyone does."

"I love you," she whispered.

He squeezed his eyes shut. He wanted to tell her she imagined it, that it was just their situation—and lust, and their history of lively debate that had prompted her imaginings. But as he debated what to say, she gathered herself enough to push away from him. A weaker woman would have turned her back to hide her feelings. Paige stood and stared at him, the bleakness in her eyes fading with each blink, until she found her center of control and lifted her chin.

"I'll see you in a little while," she said.

"Soon," he agreed, then he took the few steps he needed to leave her, and he was outside the cottage, alone and confused. He glanced at his watch. A twenty-minute walk to his house; thirty minutes until the patrol car would be there, so he took his time, enjoying the sparkling freshness of the rain-swept city.

I love you.

Damn. She'd said the words almost apologetically, certainly reluctantly.

I love you.

He'd heard those words before, but they hadn't reflected a lifelong commitment, such as his parents had had. And Kani and Iain. No, they'd meant, "I love you for the moment." For Joanna, only until death brought her peace. For Terri, only until she finally found peace after her husband's death. Neither had really wanted him, just what comfort and strength he had to offer.

I love you.

And Paige? What could he offer her that she needed? Sex? Under that prim and proper exterior was a woman who earned the sexy lingerie she liked to wear. Tonight he'd ask her to dress as she had on the plane, minus the skirt and blouse. Fantasies should be fulfilled, after all.

I love you.

Too? He shook his head, forcing away the thought. He needed to concentrate on what was ahead. He needed her to be just another assignment so that he could do his job objectively. He needed for her cameo face to stop haunting him, and her whispered words to stop echoing in his mind.

His silent pager vibrated against his waist. Startled, he dug past the jacket, yanked off the device and stared at it before he took off at a dead run.

He would have burst into the cottage had not years of caution stopped him, making him proceed carefully, listening along the walls as he tiptoed by, then again at the front door. He heard Lloyd pleading with her, saying something about waiting for Rye to return. He shoved the door open.

"Oh, thank God," Lloyd said, sagging with relief. "She's packing."

"What?" Rye swept past him, taking huge steps toward the bedroom. *"What the hell do you think you're doing?"*

"I'm going home." Simple words, simply spoken.

"Like hell you are."

She slammed a newspaper against his stomach as she strode past him to head to the bathroom. "Page three," she called out, the jumble of sounds indicating she was scooping up everything there.

Rye stared at the masthead of the *The Wall Street Journal*, then turned to page three and scanned the headlines, finding the one she obviously meant. *Boston shipping firms pen deal*. He skimmed the article. Collins-Abrahamson Shipping had merged with O'Halloran Shipping, effective this date. The new slate of officers and directors was named, a mention of price noted. He folded the paper and returned his gaze to the fuming, furious woman who was muttering obscenities and dumping cosmetics into her suitcase.

"Didn't he say the deal would be on hold until you got back?" Rye asked.

"Well, we know my father, don't we? Wait until I get my hands on him. He didn't just take advantage of my being out of Boston to finagle this deal without me. He set it up. He set everything up."

"You think you never were in danger? That it was a ploy to keep you away during negotiations?"

"Trust me. If you meet Joey Falcon, you'll understand that he's not the kind of man to get that deeply in debt with gangsters. My father used him. Used *you*, Rye. He knew I wouldn't believe anything less than your involvement."

Would Patrick have gone to such elaborate measures over a business deal? Rye wondered. "I think we should call first and check. If you're wrong, you're walking into a minefield."

"I'm not perpetuating his cowardice by confronting him over the phone. Oh, no. I'm dealing with him in person. I want to see his face when he tries to worm his way out of this one."

He cupped her arm, pulled her away from the suitcase she was trying to jam shut. Pressing on it, he latched it. "I'm almost sure you're right, but I won't take the chance that you're not. I'm going with you. First, I'll have the police swing by my house and see if the rental car is still there, then I'll contact the airlines for reservations."

"Fine. Whatever. Oh, he's gonna pay for this, big time."
Her eyes opened wide and a wicked grin tipped the corners
of her mouth. "Hold off on that call to the airlines. I'm
chartering a jet."

Thirteen

She didn't hide her anger—that's what surprised Rye the most. He followed her from the elevator to Patrick's office as she marched her way past the few employees working late. She was fuming. She was livid. She was beautiful.

That old sexist cliché rings true, after all, Rye thought. She really is beautiful when she's angry. Beyond beautiful—stunning, even. And while he enjoyed the softness in her expression after they made love, he was even more drawn to her ferocity. Every feature stood in sharp relief; there were planes and angles he hadn't known existed. She'd settle for nothing less than full bloody battle.

She didn't knock on Patrick's door but grasped the knob and slammed it open so hard it bounced off the wall. She flattened her palm against it as it flew back at her and shoved it hard again as she passed through the doorway, letting it boomerang into Rye, who slowed the trajectory and closed it quietly behind them.

Patrick jerked out of his chair. As usual, his shirt cuffs were rolled up, his tie loosened. His six-foot frame rivaled any stevedore on the docks in sinew and strength. His deep auburn hair begged to be trimmed.

A decidedly hot and heavy feel hovered in the air as father and daughter squared off. Rye settled himself on the leather sofa, leaned back and awaited the floor show, his fingers linked behind his neck, one ankle resting across the opposite knee.

Paige slapped the newspaper on Patrick's desk as he sat down again. Her curls bounced like springs with the force of her movement. "You lied."

Patrick glanced at the paper then up at Paige. "You've made some interesting changes in yourself."

"We are not discussing me. We're discussing you. This—" She stopped abruptly, catching her breath, gathering control. She jabbed the newspaper article. "This is beyond forgiveness. How could you do this to me?"

Patrick leaned back in his chair and steepled his fingers in front of his mouth; his forefingers bounced against his lips. "It was for the good of the company. I didn't do anything *to* you."

"It's a slap in the face. You've played games with me before, but this surpasses anything I would have thought you capable of. The risk to the company with this merger is—"

"Worth it," Patrick interrupted.

Rye stood and wandered closer. "I need a piece of paper, Patrick."

Father and daughter turned toward him, twin expressions of bafflement forging matching burrows between their brows.

Patrick shook his head bluntly. "What?"

"A piece of stationery, please."

Acting automatically, Patrick slid open a desk drawer, withdrew a single piece of letterhead and passed it to Rye, who uttered a cheerful thanks and retreated to the sofa again. Both O'Hallorans watched him settle down, pull out a slim gold pen from his pocket and begin writing.

Paige shook her head and returned her gaze to her father. "The move is not good for the company," she said

more calmly. "It's too big a risk. And I don't know if I can
be a part of its downfall."

"You won't be."

"You're so sure it won't be a disaster?"

Patrick rubbed his face with his hands then locked them
over his stomach. "You won't be part of it, win or lose,
Paige. Your job's been assigned to the comptroller of Collins-Abrahamson."

"You're firing me?" Rage and shock warred on her face.
She took a stumbling step backward. Rye watched Patrick
walk around his desk and try to put his hands on Paige's
arms. She brought hers up and out violently, knocking his
away.

"You're ruining my business, kid," Patrick said, his voice
tight and soft.

Paige held herself in rigid control, fighting thunderous
emotions. She started the next sentence three times before
she could get the words out. "We've had a steady eleven
percent profit in the years I've had a hand in the decisions."

"And we had twenty or thirty, even forty percent profits
in previous years."

"And some with no profit. Two with losses," Paige reminded him, her voice losing strength with each word.

"A long time ago." Again Patrick reached for her. Again
she knocked him away. "It's no fun anymore. I need to have
the fun back."

"How much were the lunches we bought at the conve-
nience store on Christmas?" Rye asked from the sofa.

Paige turned her head by jerky degrees to squint at Rye.
"What?"

"Our Christmas picnic. Do you remember how much we
paid?"

She frowned. "No. Rye, this is important."

He pointed to the paper on the low table before him.
"So's this. Sorry for the interruption," he said lightly, as-
suring himself she was under control again before letting her
face Patrick.

She exhaled a steadying breath. "You want *fun*, Dad? You've got how many employees now that you've merged with another company? People who have families, who need security and stability. Ask them if they're happy with an eleven percent almost-guaranteed profit, or a surprise every year. Ask them if they care whether the job is fun for you or not."

"Now wait a minute, Paige. You know damn well I'm not going to risk my employees' jobs. Those years we had losses, I took only enough salary to survive. I never laid off anyone. And, dammit, it *is* important whether or not I have fun." He swept an arm to indicate the room. "I'm fed up being stuck behind a desk pushing papers. I enjoy getting out on the docks and loading or unloading with the men. You know I do. I've been so tied to paperwork I haven't been able to do that. I've got employees I haven't met, who don't know me from Adam. That's not the way I built this business."

Patrick paced the room as he continued. "The merger frees me—it frees me from paperwork, from this damned room! I can go out in the field again, make deals, negotiate. I love that. I've missed it these last few years. You did a good job, Paige. But you're just too damned conservative."

"My mother would have been proud," Paige said, her voice husky.

"It's true. She would have. I have no doubt you can be a big help to a company. It's just not going to be this one."

Paige's chin came up. "I never would have suspected you were a coward, Dad. I can't believe you went to all this trouble just to finagle a deal. I *am* rational. You could have fired me without the elaborate ploy." She glanced at Rye, who smiled encouragingly. "You took valuable time from Rye's life. He could have been helping someone who really needed it. Well, I guess it's a fitting end to our rather rocky relationship, isn't it?"

Patrick flinched. "It's a *change* in our relationship, honey. In the long run, it'll probably be better for us both.

We've worked together forever. I don't even know if this is what you really wanted to do, deep in your heart.''

She laughed and tossed her head in a defensive gesture. ''What if I said I wanted to be an elephant trainer? Funny how twenty-eight years have gone by and you never asked. Now that you're feeling guilty, you take a sudden interest in my dreams.''

Rye grinned. He didn't know how serious she was, but he admired her guts. Patrick looked as if she'd slugged him in the stomach.

''You've always been first in my life, Paige.''

''*I've always been second.*'' The words were shouted; the pain came through a second later as a whisper. ''Second. Maybe even third, because the company came ahead of me, too. But I always, always came after my mother's deified memory.''

''I never—''

''*You always,*'' she countered. ''My mother, the paragon of virtue. The calm, the elegant, the perfect woman. The love of your life, even in death. I know I don't hold a candle to her, but I'm here. I'm alive. Humans make mistakes. Angels can't.''

Her pain layered a new heaviness in the air. Rye stopped referring to his notes, stopped writing on the stationery. He saw Patrick take a step back and turn from his daughter. Silently, Rye urged him to be honest with Paige for once.

''I loved your mother,'' Patrick said finally.

''You worshiped her,'' Paige corrected him. ''You wanted me to be just like her, and I can't be. I'm like you, don't you see that? I'm like you.''

''No.'' Patrick shook his head vigorously. ''You're like her. You look like her. You move like her. When you laugh— God, when you laugh, I hear her.''

''I look like her?'' Paige latched onto the words. ''But... you've always said... she was beautiful.''

''The most beautiful woman I've ever known.''

''And I look like her?''

"Almost exactly. Damn. If your mother had lived, everything would have been different. She wasn't an angel, you know. God, she was so young. So young to have the responsibility of marriage and a baby. We didn't have any idea what we were getting into. But love is so powerful. It didn't matter. Nothing mattered but each other, then you, Paige." He shook his head slowly. "We had some doozy fights. It was so much fun making up."

Paige blinked, startled. "Wait a minute. You've always talked about how quiet and soothing she was. How she kept you in line."

"I didn't want you to think your mother was a shrew, honey. She wasn't. She sparred with me, but I needed that."

Paige just stared at him. Rye could see her sorting information, aligning it with lifelong beliefs. She seemed to scan her memory banks, stopped occasionally to read the history there, then scanned some more. Trancelike, she picked up her purse from the chair she'd tossed it into; she turned and walked to the door. Once there, she swiveled to face Patrick again. Her gaze never once included Rye.

It was too much emotion for her, he could see that. She was torn between pain, disbelief and anger. She couldn't think logically, so she had to retreat for a while and pull herself together. The expression she left Patrick with said volumes.

Both men watched her leave, her dignity intact.

"You should go with her," Patrick said. "She's too upset."

"She can't drive because her car's not here." He passed through the door in time to see her disappear into an office two doors down. "Buzz your secretary and tell her to let you know if she leaves the office." He ambled in Patrick's direction as the call was made. Rye watched him hang up the phone, drop into his chair, lean his elbows on the desk and sink his head into his hands. He slid the piece of stationery into Patrick's line of vision.

Patrick's arms plopped onto the desk as he focused on the paper. "What's this?"

Rye hooked a leg over the desk corner and crossed his arms over his chest. "My bill. Itemized, as your departing comptroller requires."

"*How* much...?"

"The charter we took back here was pretty expensive. I think that's everything. If not, I'll send along an additional statement when I send the receipts," Rye said matter-of-factly. "Pretty expensive merger."

Patrick flipped the invoice into his in-basket, then ignored him.

"Do you have any idea what could have happened with this game of yours?" Rye's fury, held leashed since he'd first entered Patrick's office, finally broke free. He leaned his hands on the desk; his voice reverberated with anger and authority. "I was prepared to maim—even kill—anyone who looked at us funny. Paige and I both were spooked by anything that happened out of the ordinary and by people who were no threat to us. She could have been killed if she'd gotten too scared and started making thoughtless mistakes. *Killed.* Are you getting the picture?"

"She's always had a good head on her shoulders," Patrick said defensively.

"The most sane of people lose the ability to make rational decisions when faced with fear. Did you think this through at all?" He closed his eyes against the red haze of rage until Patrick's shaky voice drew him back.

"Obviously, not enough. I didn't mean to put her in danger. Or you."

"Right. You just wanted her out of the way so you could negotiate your deal." Rye straightened. "I can't believe you fooled me. I knew something wasn't right about this whole business, but I had decided that you were working on your own here and didn't want to distract me from watching out for Paige. I'm amazed you devised enough suspense to keep me sure of her need for protection."

"I didn't do that. You did."

"What do you mean?"

Patrick sighed. "I mean I hadn't thought of anything beyond telling Paige her house was broken into. You just kept giving me ideas when you asked questions."

"Paige told me you freaked out when you couldn't track us down on Christmas."

"I panicked. I thought for sure you'd headed back here, and we weren't signing papers until the next day."

Rye snorted. So, because he'd kept Patrick informed and asked all the right questions, the game had been perpetuated. Some kind of investigator he was. He'd been far too personally involved in this assignment. He should have known what Patrick was up to. He should have known.

Rye watched Patrick move items on his desk, one at a time, an inch at a time, then move them back, obviously uncomfortable. And maybe something else. Guilty? "Patrick," Rye said quietly, then waited until the older man looked at him. "Exactly how long have you been plotting to get Paige and me together?"

Fourteen

—

Paige sat alone in her office staring out the window. Her father was proof a person could love unconditionally, she decided. Time and again he played games with her; time and again she forgave him. She would this time, too—eventually. Maybe it was for the best, her leaving the company. Maybe she'd do better elsewhere, where her performance was the only criterion for success.

It's only a job, she thought with a shrug that she recognized more as bravado than acceptance. What intrigued her most was Patrick's assertion she looked like her mother. Maybe that was one of their problems. Maybe he couldn't be rational with her because she was a visible reminder of loss. Maybe he couldn't ever be free to find another woman to love with Paige around.

Then there was Rye—yet another pawn on Patrick's chessboard.

So much had happened between them over the course of six days. The threat of danger had heightened tension and exaggerated dependency. With danger no longer a factor, their time together was taking on a surrealistic quality. Reality could swing a vicious blow to emotions, she decided as she tried to sort out her feelings.

Was any of it real? The unfamiliar sense of anticipation he'd aroused in her over the phone for two years? The discovery of a woman inside her she hadn't ever acknowledged—one who was earthy and adventurous? The things they'd done together might have shocked her if she hadn't been so immersed in the pleasure of it all. Was that enough?

A knock interrupted her musings. She turned her chair around as the door opened. Rye stood framed in the doorway. They shared a brief look before he shut the door.

She watched him scan her office, then he took a seat opposite her, across the desk.

"How are you?" he asked.

"Dandy." She leaned back and folded her arms over her stomach.

"Are you ready to go home? Should I call a cab for us?"

"I think I'm just going to box up my personal things now and take them with me. I don't really want to come back."

"Won't there be a transition of—"

"Power?" she interrupted. "That wouldn't include me, would it? He can figure it out. So can they. My system is easy to follow."

"What will you do?"

Die a little. She pushed herself out of the chair and turned her back on him to stare out the window again. He wasn't saying what she wanted to hear. She'd told him this morning that she loved him. There was no way he could have missed hearing it. "Maybe I'll go to Hawaii for a week. Sleep, enjoy some sun, do some reading."

She felt him come up behind her.

"That was my plan, too. Do you want company?"

She closed her eyes. Wishful thinking was a dangerous thing. She had to be very careful that she knew what he was asking. "That depends."

"On what?"

"Your reasons for wanting to go together."

She felt his hands settle on her shoulders. "We've got something pretty great going. I don't want it to end."

"And after the week is over, what then, Rye?"

His hands tightened. "We deal with that then."

Die now or die later. She pulled away from him, making a decision. It was obvious he didn't return her love. "I don't want to diminish what we shared. I'd rather have just the memories of a few perfect days than try to keep alive what would soon enough die a natural death."

"Why do you think it would die?"

His tone was neutral, one business contact to another. If he didn't get out of here in a minute she was going to throw herself at him and start begging. He would hate that as much as she would. "Because you're not ready for commitment, and I've decided that I am. I think that along with job hunting, I'll do a little husband hunting."

His brows drew into a deep V. "You're not serious."

They stood a foot apart, gazes locked, bodies stiff. "You gave me a taste of what it could be like. I want more."

"Come with me to Hawaii. We haven't scratched the surface of what there can be, Paige."

She shook her head. "As wonderful as it was, I just can't."

"Are you testing yourself again?"

"Maybe. It's probably better if we don't see each other, or talk to each other for a while."

He shoved a hand through his hair and turned away.

Tell me you love me, she begged him silently.

He said nothing, and in that she found her answers.

"Tell Lloyd I said goodbye," she said, forcing control into the words.

"Dammit! You can't let it just end like this."

"You heard my father. I'm just too damned conservative. I tend to cut my losses before they end in bankruptcy. Thank you for—"

"Stuff it," he said, low and angry. "I don't want or need your gratitude."

"Then there's nothing left to say." *Get out, get out, get out.*

He took a few steps, rested his hand on the doorknob and his forehead against the door. His words were directed to the floor. "If our birth control failed, you will let me know?"

Paige felt blindly for the corner of her desk as her knees buckled. She hadn't seriously considered it. A baby? Rye's baby? Unconsciously, she flattened a hand to her abdomen.

"Promise me."

He had turned to face her, had caught her with her fingers splayed protectively across her belly. She nodded.

"It's been a hell of a trip, Harry."

Her lips quivered in some semblance of a smile. She lifted her chin. "To the ends of the earth and back, Warner."

A moment later he was gone. She found if she concentrated on individual muscles, she could move to her chair and lower herself into it. Slumping, she fought reacting to the loss, knowing she was reverting to old habits, habits she intended to change as soon as she left her father's company and began a new life.

Rye punched a button on the elevator panel then leaned against the wall, closing his eyes for the few seconds it took to reach the lobby. He stepped out into eerie quiet. As his footsteps sounded on the marble floor, he listened to the steady rhythm and heard the slight creak of leather. Suddenly chilled, he stopped walking to shrug into the leather jacket he carried loosely in one hand. Glancing through the plate glass floor-to-ceiling windows, he saw that it was snowing.

Mechanically, he fastened each snap of his jacket. He moved forward two steps, then stopped. Leaning so that his body would be forced to follow, he took two more, then stopped. One. Stop. Jamming his hands into his jacket pockets, he frowned at his feet as they seemed glued to the floor. The hollowness of the room echoed the ragged sound of his breathing.

"Damn." The word bounced wall to wall, floor to ceiling. "Damn."

She'd let him go. No tears, no begging, no compromises. She'd said she loved him, then she'd let him walk away. She'd asked nothing of him.

Nothing. He looked ahead at his life and saw nothing. *So, now who's the vulnerable one?*

He spotted a bench and moved there to sit. Resting his forearms on his thighs, he clasped his hands together and bowed his head. Images of her swam in his mind—cool and controlled, belligerent, playful. Hugging Lloyd. Holding his niece in her arms. Glorying in their lovemaking.

She'd said she loved him. Then she let him go.

Maybe knowing about her father's deception made a difference in how she felt. Maybe everything was changed now. She wore her armor differently than he did, hiding behind control while he hid behind strength. Couldn't she have shown him just a little vulnerability, a little weakness, a little dependency?

He blew out a breath and leaned back against the wall to stare at the ceiling. No, she couldn't have. It was one of the things he loved about her.

Just one of the things.

Paige caught a movement from the corner of her eye and turned to see a white handkerchief being waved through the crack of her almost closed door.

"Cease-fire?" Patrick called.

"You own the building."

He pushed open the door and shoved the white square into a back pocket. "Where's Rye?"

"Gone." She tried to let him know with her expression that she didn't want to talk about it, that she'd crumble if she even had to say his name.

His lips tightened momentarily. "I guess you're pretty ticked off at me," he said at last.

"If you're into understatement, that would about cover it. But it's dying fast."

"Why?"

"Because it will be better for our relationship if we don't work together anymore."

"I was actually right once? And you're admitting it?"

She smiled as he sat down. "I guess I deserved that. I've been pretty unyielding myself."

"Sounds like you mean to change that."

"I do." She picked up a round crystal paperweight and hefted it lightly in her hand. But it reminded her of weights, which reminded her of the gym...which reminded her of what she'd lost. She set the object carefully on her desk.

"I need to come clean with you, kid," Patrick said.

"About what?"

"About Rye. I, uh, sort of picked him out for you."

"Picked him out?" The words came out one at a time, disbelief layering each syllable.

He stood and shoved his hands in his pockets. "A long time ago—long before you were ready for a man like him. But when you fell so fast for Joey Falcon, I knew I couldn't wait any longer. He came to me, demanding money."

"So that much was true," Paige said.

"I threw him out on his ear, but it made me pay attention. It wasn't only that you'd gotten involved in a shipboard romance, but also because you just up and left on a spur-of-the-moment trip. Falcon wasn't a good choice for you, but you developed some kind of attraction to him anyway. Obviously, your hormones were in overdrive." His face flushed as he looked away from her. "I decided if you were in the mating mood, you should be within range of Rye."

"Dad!"

"Believe me, it wasn't easy for me to do. You're still my little girl, you know."

She smiled at his discomfort. "You never were comfortable talking to me about the facts of..." Her words drifted into silence as she saw looming in her open doorway a man who could have understudied Arnold Schwarzenegger in *Conan the Barbarian*.

"Leave us alone, please, Patrick," Rye said, not looking at the man but at Paige.

"Now, hold on—"

"Dad. It's all right." She returned Rye's penetrating stare. Anticipation battled hope at the look on his face "I'll be fine."

She didn't notice her father leaving, she just knew when he was gone. She locked her hands together on her desktop and waited as Rye came all the way into the office and closed the door. He walked around her desk, turned her chair toward him and crouched before her.

"I have a proposition for you."

Wariness clouded her hope. "What?"

He reached into his pocket, pulled out his business card and passed it to her. He had drawn a line through his name and penned in Paige O'Halloran.

"You're offering me a *job?*" She crushed the card then threw it over his shoulder. "Don't do me any favors. I don't need your pity."

"Pity? Offering you an exciting job with more adventure than you could imagine amounts to pity?"

She waved a negligent hand. "You're a protector. You also feel an obligation to me because of . . . what we shared. What work could I possibly do for you? Run a computer, do your billing?"

"Well, my accounting system does need an overhaul—"

"Go to hell."

She said the words with saccharine sweetness, and he ducked his head, hiding his relief that she'd turned down the offer.

"Hmm. If that job offer doesn't appeal to you, how about this one?" He tugged two more business cards out of his pocket and laid them side by side on her desk.

Paige noted his hands were shaking. She glanced at his face, registered the uncertainty there, then looked at the cards. The distinctive logo of Warner Investigations once more caught her eye. However, instead of crossing out his name and just replacing it with hers, he'd written Paige O'Halloran-Warner on one and Paige Warner on the other.

"I have to tell you," he said, sinking onto his knees, "that the responsibilities are a little different with this offer. And the perks. You can choose any of the three offers, but I much prefer either the second or third. It's your choice entirely."

Paige swallowed. "Why?"

"Because I know that name choice is an issue these days—"

She sliced her hand through the air, cutting him off. "Why are you offering me this at all?"

"Because I love you, Harry."

She squeezed her eyes shut as her throat closed for an instant. "Why?"

He clasped her hands and waited until she looked at him. "Because you love and accept Lloyd. Because you swagger in motorcycle leathers. Because you like garter belts and flannel pajamas and you don't even own a bra."

She started to cry, and he drew her forward to lay her head on his shoulder. "You need more? I love you because you have a fascinating mind and because you have curly hair and long legs and a great . . . tush." He slid his hands down her, cupped her bottom and lifted her to sit her on the desk. He leaned a hand on each side of her, his wrists pressing against her thighs. "And perfect breasts with nipples that beg—"

"Beg?" She flattened her hands against his cheeks.

"Beg. Just for me."

Her face felt hot. "Beyond the physical, you believe we have enough to make it for a lifetime? Because I won't accept anything less."

"Harry, you're a jigsaw puzzle to me, one I can't find all the border pieces for. You only let me work from the middle outward—do you know how hard that is to do? It's going to *take* a lifetime to find where all the pieces go. And then I still have to frame the edge. I'm looking forward to it. More than I can tell you."

He pulled her desk chair under him to sit down. "Now, it's your turn," he said, squeezing her hands.

Her gaze softened. "I love you."

"Tell me why."

She tipped back her head and laughed. "Because you wear Goofy socks. Because you actually believe you're a feminist. Because you love Lloyd, and you cried when you held your niece." She looped her hands around his neck and caressed his face with her eyes. "Because when you made love to me, you didn't take what I offered lightly, but accepted it as a responsibility. Because you never complained about having to wear a condom, and because you saw what a pathetic creature I was and made adventures for me."

"I never saw you as pathetic, just restrained. And I knew underneath that prim and proper exterior lived a woman who was dying to break free. I'd heard a different you on the phone, and a little garter convinced me of the rest." He glanced at the door. "Do you think Patrick is gone? Should we invite him in and tell him the news?"

"I think we should lock the door and celebrate." She wriggled forward.

"No protection," he said apologetically.

"Wrong. I kept one as a memento." She picked up her purse from the desk and pulled out a packet and a brass shell casing. "This, too. Don't look at me like that. I didn't have theater stubs or flowers, did I?"

His mouth quirked as he stood. "I think we should check on your father—"

She practically scaled his body to kiss him. Her arms twined and retwined around him as she moved against him. Hot, hungry mouths took and gave fiercely. When she couldn't align herself closely enough, she pulled him to the floor with her.

"We can't do this, Harry. Patrick—"

"I know," she groaned as she lifted her hips toward him.

He rolled off her to lay beside her, ordering his body to stop throbbing. "How big is your bed?"

"Big enough," she said with a grating chuckle. She curled her fingers around his fist. "I don't know if I can get past my gag reflex to actually tell my father that he was right, and thank you so very much."

Rye suddenly snapped his fingers. "I think I know just the woman for him." He rolled to his side and laughed. "First time he comes to visit, we'll arrange it."

"He won't like us playing matchmaker."

"You'd like a happy ending for your father, too, wouldn't you?"

"Is that your goal, or do you want him to suffer for his own games?"

"Why would I punish the man who made sure I got the one person in the world meant for me?"

Paige smiled. "So why do I see a gleam in your eyes? Are you really thinking of me, or of revenge?"

His eyes sparkled with innocence. "Of you, Harry. Only of you."

* * * * *

COMING NEXT MONTH

#955 WILDCAT—Rebecca Brandewyne

October's *Man of the Month*, wildcatter Morgan McCain, wanted every inch of city slicker Cat Devlin, but there was no way he was going to let her womanly wiles lure love into his hardened heart.

#956 A WOLF IN THE DESERT—BJ James

Men of the Black Watch

Patience O'Hara knew she was in trouble when she felt more than fear for her dangerously handsome kidnapper. What was it about Matthew Winter Sky that had her hoping her rescue would never come?

#957 THE COWBOY TAKES A LADY—Cindy Gerard

One night with irresistible Sara Stewart had rough-and-tough cowboy Tucker Lambert running for cover. Because falling for Sara would mean saying "I do" for this confirmed bachelor!

#958 A WIFE IN TIME—Cathie Linz

Kane Wilder was driving Susannah Hall crazy! But when they were both sent back in time to solve a mystery, Susannah's only chance for survival was to pose as the stubborn man's wife....

#959 THE BACHELOR'S BRIDE—Audra Adams

Marry Reid James? No way! But Rachel Morgan's pregnancy left her no choice but to accept the infuriating man's proposal—even if it was *just* for her baby....

#960 THE ROGUE AND THE RICH GIRL—Christine Pacheco

Premiere

Prim and proper Nicole Jackson was desperate, and hotshot Ace Lawson was the only man who could help her. Now if she could only be sure he would never discover her secret....

Take 4 bestselling love stories FREE

Plus get a FREE surprise gift!

Become a Privileged Woman,
You'll be entitled to all these Free Benefits. And Free Gifts, too.

To thank you for buying our books, we've designed an exclusive FREE program called *PAGES & PRIVILEGES™*. You can enroll with just one Proof of Purchase, and get the kind of luxuries that, until now, you could only read about.

BIG HOTEL DISCOUNTS

A privileged woman stays in the finest hotels. And so can you—at up to 60% off! Imagine standing in a hotel check-in line and watching as the guest in front of you pays $150 for the same room that's only costing you $60. Your *Pages & Privileges* discounts are good at Sheraton, Marriott, Best Western, Hyatt and thousands of other fine hotels all over the U.S., Canada and Europe.

FREE DISCOUNT TRAVEL SERVICE

A privileged woman is always jetting to romantic places.

When <u>you</u> fly, just make one phone call for the lowest published airfare at time of booking— <u>or double the difference back!</u>

PLUS—you'll get a $25 voucher to use the first time you book a flight AND <u>5% cash back on every ticket you buy thereafter through the travel service!</u>

PROOF OF PURCHASE
Offer expires October 31, 1996

SD-PP59